'I'm in trouble...

'I've had that strong [...] in St. Mary's a week [...] felt I must find out w[...] involved in, before something wors[...]

'That's why you tried so hard to get rid of me?' Karen asked. 'Because you didn't want me to get involved in whatever it was?'

Judd nodded. 'I'm in deeper than I thought. You know the police will be back. I've already wasted too much time when I could have been searching for the truth.'

Karen didn't hesitate. 'I'll get my clothes on and we can go.'

'There's no need for you to come with me.'

She circled the table and put her arms around his neck. 'Do you want the truth or do you want to be Rambo?'

He snorted, but sensed his resolve softening.

'Then take me with you,' she whispered, her mouth close to his ear...

Dear Reader

Welcome to Intrigue™! This month brings you the last in the fabulous **McCullar Brothers** series, *Remember My Touch*. Husband and wife Mac and Jenny McCullar had never doubted they'd be together—until Mac was killed. But five years later, Jenny meets rugged stranger Matt Dawson, and something in her just seems to welcome him home...

Meanwhile, in *Only a Memory Away*, Judd Maxwell's only connection with his past is a recurring nightmare about running from the law. Social worker Karen Thomas is trying to help him uncover the truth, but what if he is guilty of a crime he doesn't even remember?

The heroes of our next two books are equally enigmatic. In *Never Cry Wolf*, Donovan Wilde meets Laurel Newkirk, who claims she is engaged to him. He knows she has the wrong man—but who is impersonating him and why? While in *Priority Male*, Rand Sinclair is the only one who can help Jasmine Ross uncover her family's secrets, and protect her from their attempts to silence her...

Enjoy them all!

The Editors

Only a Memory Away

MADELINE ST. CLAIRE

SILHOUETTE

INTRIGUE

All the characters in this book have no existence outside the imagination of the author, and have no relation whatsoever to anyone bearing the same name or names. They are not even distantly inspired by any individual known or unknown to the author, and all the incidents are pure invention.

Silhouette and Colophon are registered trademarks of Harlequin Books S.A., used under licence.

*First published in Great Britain 1999
Silhouette Books, Eton House, 18-24 Paradise Road,
Richmond, Surrey TW9 1SR*

© Leslie Carpentiers 1998

ISBN 0 373 22484 2

46-9906

*Printed and bound in Spain
by Litografia Rosés S.A., Barcelona*

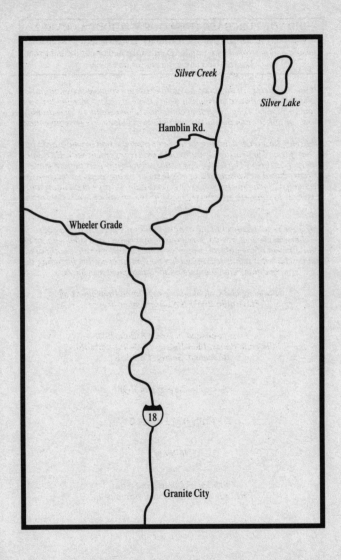

This book is dedicated
in loving memory to my mother,
Jaquith Juin Croker

Chapter One

Marlene Hall had no plans to die that mild August night.

Rather the reverse. All that final Friday, the young woman had been thinking about her future. If she slowed down and thought with her head instead of her heart, she was sure she could figure out the right solution to her problems.

And then her man came, and made her last decision for her.

Quickly, desperately, but efficiently, he stole her future from her. Then tried to cover his guilt beneath the pine needles and acid soil of a lonely mountain forest.

It was hard labor. When the murderer was finished, he felt exhausted, like someone who in an extreme emergency had lifted a car with his bare hands.

Looking up through the trees, he realized the moon had risen while he worked. He doused the flashlight and stuck it in his belt. On the long walk back to the road, he tried to wipe the grime from his palms, comparing himself to Judas.

What a ghastly thing he had done! It had been necessary; he must never doubt that she had given him no other choice. But how ugly it was. Could he ever erase the pictures from his mind? He would *have* to, if he was to go on living. Yes, he must will himself, with every ounce of his considerable intellect, to forget.

He found his vehicle where he had left it, in an abandoned lane that led to a disintegrating summer cabin. With force he pulled the car door shut, marking it as an outward sign of his inward decision. He was closing his mind on the other women and on Marlene Hall, the obsessive relationships—everything that had led him here. The powerful thought comforted him, relaxed him. He leaned deeper into the seat, let the engine run. He suddenly felt drowsy, almost peaceful. Pity it was such a long drive back to Silver Creek. He felt as though he could drift off right here, and sleep for hours.

"KAREN, I'VE FOUND the *perfect* man for you!"

Karen couldn't see through the telephone line, but she knew her old friend from high school like a book. Vivian was doing her best to sound excited but sincere. In truth, both of them knew she was teasing.

"Really? Tell me," Karen said. There was no reason to spoil Viv's fun, even at her own expense.

"Remember, when we had lunch last week, you said you wished more than anything you could find a man without a past? Well, this is the guy."

"Hmm. Only *one* ex-wife, right?"

"No, none."

"No addiction to alcohol, drugs or his own image in the mirror?"

Vivian chuckled. "Uh-uh. He doesn't even smoke."

"He's not openly, secretly or as yet undecidedly gay?"

A pause, then slowly Vivian answered, "*Definitely* not."

Karen pictured her friend's arched eyebrow, the tip of Viv's tongue tracing her upper teeth. *So this guy was a real hunk?* Genuine interest sparked in Karen, but she kept her tone skeptical in case Viv was only leading her on.

"No history," Karen asked, "of 'searching for himself' using the indiscriminate, low-paying job sampling method?"

"If you don't believe me, why don't you ask him yourself? He's dining at the hospital tonight, if you want to meet him."

"The hospital? Another doctor? No thanks, no more type-A's, *please.*"

"He's not a doctor, Karen…he's a patient."

"A *patient?*" Vivian worked in the psychiatric ward at St. Mary's. "In *your* department?"

Smothered laughter came across the line. Drat it, Vivian had gotten her. "Okay, okay. You've fixed me up with Norman Bates. What's this all about?"

"No, Karen, nothing like that. No psychos. Oh…" Vivian stopped laughing and audibly drew a breath.

At last she's going to get serious, Karen thought.

"He's an amnesiac."

AS KAREN DROVE to her appointment with Judd Maxwell the following afternoon at three, she wondered if she was going crazy.

Vivian had been kidding, of course, about a possible romance with the mysterious mental patient. Still, his story had been intriguing. A gorgeous thirty-three-year-old man found in a kind of trance, parked in the trees just off a deserted stretch of Highway 18. Unable to recall where he'd been going or how he'd gotten there, or even who he was. There was nothing in the auto to identify the man but the vehicle registration: a resultant search of Department of Motor Vehicle records revealed nothing more than his vital statistics and a defunct post-office box address in faraway Los Angeles. The highway patrol speculated that Maxwell had blacked out for some reason, and then been robbed of his wallet and other valuables by some opportunistic thief. The HP had spotted Maxwell slumped in the driver's seat and stopped to investigate around midnight last Friday.

As administrative assistant to the chief of psychiatry at St. Mary's in Granite City, it had been Vivian's job to contact the social services department and request they transfer Judd into the state system since he apparently had no health insurance and the private hospital couldn't keep him on. However, it had been Vivian's idea to call her good friend, social worker Karen Thomas, direct rather than going through the usual channels.

As Karen paused for a downtown traffic light, she fiddled with the Ford Festiva's air conditioner, absently wishing she'd gotten the AC serviced before this record-breaking heat wave. She frowned, more at her impulsiveness than the oppressive humidity, remembering that she'd felt instant sympathy for the amnesiac and for how alone and terrified he must feel. She hadn't thought twice about acting on Vivian's suggestion that she press the county social services director to assign her as Maxwell's social worker. The director had agreed, saying the case shouldn't be unusually difficult: find the man a place to stay, perhaps in a men's halfway house; get him a referral to the county mental-health clinic; monitor his progress until his memory returned.

But after Karen had had some time to think, she had begun to realize how much simple, base curiosity was mixed with her desire to help Judd Maxwell. And the closer she got to her appointment with Judd and his attending psychiatrist, Dr. Bergman, the more ashamed she felt for indulging her curiosity, and the more apprehensive.

She needed no reminding that in the two years she'd worked in the mountain community since getting her master's degree, most of her clients had been senior citizens. The needs of the indigent elderly was her area of expertise; Alzheimer's disease and senile dementia were the closest she'd come to dealing with mental problems. She'd never had a real psych case before, or a male client under age seventy, not to mention someone afflicted with total amnesia, for goodness' sake.

Karen turned into the parking lot in front of the hospital and began searching for a space as she fought off a wave of nerves. Time was growing short, and she still wasn't sure how she should go about establishing rapport with her new client. Vivian had described Judd as coherent but uncommunicative when the nurses brought him his meals. *Not* reassuring.

Karen pulled her car into a slot and grabbed her purse and a 35mm camera off the seat. She had thought that perhaps an offer to take Judd's photo, to run it in the local newspaper, would break the ice. As she slung the camera strap over her shoulder and headed for the main doors, she pictured herself extending the camera to a befuddled Judd so he could see it. "If you have friends or relatives in the area, they'll see your photo in the paper and come forward to claim you."

Oh, right, putting it that way would make the poor man feel like a lost piece of luggage! If she didn't get a grip, she'd make a fool of herself and end up hurting the patient more than helping him.

The faint pneumatic whoosh of the hospital's automatic doors sounded ahead of her. The glass pocket doors slid slowly apart, then burst wide as arms of steel shoved them to the sides. A wild man exploded through the opening. Karen jumped aside a second before the tall, dark figure nearly mowed her down.

She caught a flash of his angry face—eyes hooded like an eagle's, jaw grinding. She doubted he even saw her. He strode quickly toward the street. In shock from the near collision, she stared at his leather-clad back, longish hair rippling like black waves over his collar.

Karen hitched her purse higher on her shoulder as she wondered what episode had set the stranger off. Had he just gotten the doctor's report that a loved one was terminally ill, or been fired from some job within the hospital? When he bypassed the parking lot, heading for the street, she felt relieved. It would be dangerous for someone in such a state to take the wheel of a car.

The automatic doors, amazingly, still functioned. She walked through into the coolness of the lobby, and was almost run over a second time.

Vivian catapulted toward her, caught Karen by the

forearms and gripped hard. "Did you see him? Did he go out the front?"

"You mean the man who just—"

"Come on, Karen, we've got to catch him." Vivian dragged her toward the entrance. "It's your new client, Judd Maxwell. He just had an awful fight with Dr. Bergman, and if we don't catch him, he'll completely disappear out there."

Galvanized by duty, Karen sprinted for the street, her flat shoes and slacks-clad legs carrying her faster than Vivian's high heels and narrow skirt. Karen shaded her eyes with her hand and swiveled her head both ways as Viv caught up with her on the sidewalk.

"Do you see him?"

Karen scanned the small park across the street. "Darn it, no. Let's try the corner."

The old hospital was situated in the heart of what had become over the years a congested downtown area. The two women bobbed up and down as they tried to see over the heads of the passing pedestrians.

"I knew it," Viv wailed, "he's vanished, like a needle in a haystack."

"There's still a chance we can find him. I'll run back and get my car. Wait here in case he doubles back."

When they were together in the car, Karen asked, "Any idea which way he'd go?"

"None. He still hasn't gotten his memory back."

"Well, let's try circling the hospital first. What in the heck happened this afternoon?"

"Another failed hypnosis session. Dr. Bergman and Judd tried their best, but he never succeeded in going under."

"That's not unusual, is it?"

Vivian's gaze swept the sidewalks in front of the little shops and eateries as she answered. "No, there are plenty of patients who don't respond, especially if they're strong willed. Dr. Bergman tried to convince him to not give up, but I guess Judd got impatient and thought the doctors were wasting his time. That's when the argument started. I didn't hear it all, because the head nurse went in with them and shut the door behind her. But pretty soon Judd burst out and demanded to be released. Dr. Bergman had no legal right to hold him, so they buzzed him through."

"Hmm." Karen thought she already knew the answer to her next question. "Did the doctor ask you to follow him?"

"No, that was my idea. The medical staff might be ticked off at his behavior, but *I* couldn't let him just take off, could I?"

Karen smiled. "You should have been a social worker, Viv, not a medical secretary."

"I know." Vivian sighed. "You'd better turn here or you'll run into a one-way street."

"Okay." Karen's hopes were fading; they'd circled the hospital within a two-block radius with no sign of Judd. Nonetheless she said, "In case we find him, you'd better tell me everything you know about his condition."

"Well, Dr. Bergman submitted his preliminary workup to the chief this morning, and I just *happened* to overhear them discussing it." The two women exchanged a grin. "They're sure now the amnesia wasn't caused by concussion or some other physical problem, so it must be what they call psychogenic in nature. That's the kind of amnesia you get when something so traumatic happens to you, you can't consciously face it. Forgetting the incident is like an overload protector.''

Karen was fascinated. ''But you said he'd forgotten *everything* about his past, not just whatever scared him to death.''

''It's complicated, but it has to do with the way the mind is divided. Judd has lost all episodic memory, memories of his personal life, along with the triggering episode, but he's still got what they call his skills-and-knowledge memory intact. When they asked him who the president is, he remembered, but he couldn't tell them anything about his own family, stuff like that. And he's got no idea what he did for a living, but the chief says if Judd was a carpenter, for instance, he could probably pick up a hammer and frame a house, no problem.''

''Is there anything the doctors can do, besides hypnosis, to help him get his memory back?'' Karen asked.

''I don't know. I think they were going to recommend some other form of psychotherapy if the hypnosis didn't work. Frankly, I think the docs were surprised he hadn't started regaining his memory on his own. This is Tuesday, and the blackout occurred last Friday.''

A DISCOURAGED KAREN dropped Vivian off at the hospital. They'd searched for two hours, but Judd Maxwell had simply disappeared.

It was nearly five o'clock; Karen saw no point in returning to the office. She was getting painfully tired of eating alone at home every night, so she told herself she might as well stop for dinner before starting the commute home to Silver Creek. From the pay phone at a fast food restaurant she called her supervisor; as usual, he was still in.

Her boss told her Maxwell was a fool to have taken off like that, but it wasn't Karen's fault and she shouldn't feel badly about it. Karen hung up, wondering if the director had detected in her voice the worry she'd tried to conceal. It was a waste of emotional energy, of course, fretting about Maxwell's fate. Though she never wanted to become callous, as some social workers inevitably did, she was beginning to wish she could toughen up a bit. She'd been told by several sources that a little more professional detachment would make her work easier, and she believed it.

She ate a broiled chicken burger and a diet cola, charmed by the presence of an adorable little baby and his young parents at the next table. But as she started home in the still sweltering heat, her thoughts returned to her almost-client. And five miles outside Granite, as she pumped gas into her car, a dark man with a long stride passed, walking on the verge of the road.

He didn't glance at the lone car in the service station, just kept going, a leather jacket slung over his shoulder.

Karen was puzzled. Maxwell's hair had been long and flowing, while this man's was well above the collar, his longish bangs slicked straight back off his forehead. And the wraparound sunglasses he wore hid his eyes. Still, after furtively examining him a moment, she was almost sure it was Judd Maxwell. The jeans and scarred work boots she couldn't recall exactly, but she remembered clearly the worn bomber jacket he carried.

Karen quickly paid the attendant and pulled back onto the deserted, two-lane mountain highway. That long stride of Maxwell's was eating up the road: he'd gotten farther ahead in a few minutes than she would have thought. She slowed, then carefully pulled off onto the shoulder beside him. But he kept walking. She inched the car along; he kept going. She couldn't see his head, just the tanned forearms beneath the rolled-up white shirtsleeves. Oh dear, perhaps he was in a trance again. She drove forward ten feet, stopped and rolled down the passenger's side window.

When she stuck her head out, the man was obliged to slow down. "Need a lift?" she called, trying to sound friendly and unthreatening.

Maxwell grimaced and came straight for her. Something in the determined way he moved made her draw back inside. He planted his broad palms on the windowsill and ducked to pin her with a stare.

Even with the haircut, she recognized the flinty expression and the angular jaw with its two-day growth of beard. This was definitely the juggernaut from the hospital. The opaque dark glasses only heightened his aura of menace. For a moment, she felt just like Janet Leigh facing the threatening state trooper in *Psycho*.

"No thanks," Maxwell said and drew back.

Karen dismissed her unease with the thought that outward appearances were usually deceiving. She'd had proud clients before who resisted aid when it was first offered. Maxwell was alone in an unfamiliar world, desperately needing her help, and she couldn't let him walk away.

"Hot evening," she said loudly.

Maxwell paused, one hand resting on the sill as the cicadas thrummed in the trees. Karen felt her damp blouse peel away from the vinyl seat as she leaned forward to try to catch his gaze. "They say it went over a hundred today. Where are you headed?"

He hesitated, leaned down, solemnly searched her face for a moment. Karen kept her smile pasted on, wondering if she looked as witless as she felt.

Finally he said, "Silver Creek."

"That's just where I'm going! I live in Silver Creek." Maybe if she shared something about herself, it would put him at ease. "I work in Granite." Darn. She wasn't usually so tongue-tied, but she couldn't think of anything else to say about herself without revealing her errand. "It's about, ah, thirty miles from here to Silver Creek."

"I know."

"You *know?*"

Maxwell shrugged. "The road sign, back there."

Of course. Karen kicked herself. Maxwell was frowning again. He might not have a memory, but she'd bet he was sharp. She was sure he smelled a rat and was about to tell her to get lost.

She opened her mouth to wish him a good day, but he opened the door and folded his body into her car. Karen was tall for a woman and found the tiny Festiva a bit confining, but Maxwell's head positively brushed the roof.

He'd been sweating in the heat, and a strong, not objectionable, but definitely potent and primitive masculine odor wrapped itself around Karen. His jeans revealed hard, muscular thighs and narrow hips, while his gradually widening chest and broad shoulders outspanned the seat back. He reminded her of an anaconda, six foot two inches of slender bones and rippling muscle.

She'd never been this close to such a dangerous, and devastatingly attractive, man. She felt woozy, as though his proximity had shot her blood pressure up.

Definitely *not* her usual type of client. No siree. Karen resisted the urge to punctuate her thoughts with a whistle. Don't worry, you can handle it, she told herself as she steered the car back onto the road.

Straining to sound casual, she asked, "Do you live in Silver Creek?"

He folded his arms and grunted, looked out the window. The gestures seemed more defensive than threatening. He was probably feeling vulnerable. Perfectly understandable. Karen relaxed a bit. They drove in silence for a few minutes.

"I've lived in Silver Creek all my life," she ventured. "I don't remember seeing you around."

He didn't move, didn't respond. Poor man. He seemed so...alone. There must be some way to get him to talk, to open up and admit he was in trouble.

She asked him a few more leading questions, but got nowhere, and her frustration grew. She couldn't just drive him to Silver Creek in silence and let him out to wander off alone again.

Karen took a deep breath. It might not be the most subtle way to get his attention, but she was fresh out of bright ideas. She took her eyes from the straightaway to watch his averted face. "My name is Karen Thomas. I, ah, don't know quite how to put this, Mr. Maxwell, but I know who you are."

Chapter Two

"I know who you are, too, Karen Thomas," Judd Maxwell said.

Of the several responses she'd anticipated, this wasn't one of them. The quiet way he said it, and his cold, level gaze, were intimidating. An involuntary shiver crept between her shoulders.

Karen thought quickly. She was positive she'd never met Judd Maxwell before. He wasn't the kind of man she'd forget. The answer, therefore, was simple.

"They told you about me at the hospital," she said.

"No, I don't recall anyone mentioning you."

Karen's brow furrowed. "Then what can you possibly know about me?"

Judd waved a hand. "Forget I said it."

"No. You meant it. Tell me."

Judd sighed. "All right. You were born in Silver Creek, though you went away to college. You work for the state social services department, with the public, in a low-paying job. You live at 815 G Street, you're single and you own a cat."

Karen's head whirled. Was he a mind reader? The

ridiculous thought struck her that the amnesia might have given him some strange, telepathic powers.

Maxwell twisted in the seat to face her. "I knew I'd startle you. Just so you don't think I'm some kind of stalker, I'll explain.

"I'm not in the habit, at least I don't think I am, of accepting rides from just anyone. So when your car first pulled up, I took a good look. The parking sticker on the back says social services, but there was no reserved slot number and your car is older, so I deduced you're an underling who doesn't pull much of a salary. It also figures, if you know who I am, you must be some kind of social worker sent to take me off the hospital's hands."

Karen blushed a little but said, "I'm afraid you're right on the money."

"To even get your foot in the door for a job like that, you'd need a degree. Granite is small for a county seat, and I'd be surprised if there's a four-year college within driving distance of here—therefore, you'd have to leave home to attend school. You told me yourself you've lived in Silver Creek all your life, so the chances are overwhelming you were born there.

"As for your address, your purse is open." He indicated the bag between their seats. "I could have added that you're very trusting. Anyway, your checkbook is open, too, and I can read the address and phone number on the top check. Yours is the only name printed, so I assume you're unmarried."

Karen smiled. "I thought you knew because I don't wear a ring."

"You're right. I should have thought of that."

"And the last thing you said, what was it? About

my cat?'' She thought a moment, then pointed to her leg. ''The cat hair on my slacks, right?''

He spread his hands. ''You see, there's no big mystery to it.''

''I didn't have time for the clothes brush before I left this morning.'' Karen chuckled. After the earlier tension, it felt good, and Maxwell seemed to have thawed out a bit as she'd listened to him with rapt attention. He seemed much more human now, though his powers of observation were impressive.

''Too bad I can't work the same magic on myself,'' he muttered beneath his breath.

Karen's heart went out to him. ''I'd like to help you regain your memory, if I can.''

He shook his head. ''I appreciate the lift, and your offer, but no, thanks. I wasted four days in the hospital, hanging on the doctors' assurances they could help me remember, and that was long enough. I've got a strong feeling I'll do far better on my own.''

''But where are you going to stay?''

''I'll find someplace, and the more I see of the country, the better chance I'll have of jogging my memory.''

Karen glanced at him and saw an urgent light in his eyes. It seemed like a stupid question, but growing frustration prompted her to ask it. ''What's your hurry?''

Judd didn't answer immediately. Without appearing to, he took a few moments to study persistent Karen Thomas more closely. The red curls were slightly damp about her rounded face, but she was surprisingly pretty, fresh and enthusiastic considering the oppressive heat, which would have wilted most women. His first impressions of her character were that she was a softhearted and feminine woman, a do-gooder by choice, motivated by what was probably an inborn desire to help other people. He still thought that, but he wondered now if she wasn't also more intelligent, more perceptive, than he'd judged at first. And that meant it was time to get rid of her.

He clenched his teeth as the driven feeling pressed on him again. He must recover his memory as quickly as possible. What fueled his apprehension, he couldn't say. It might be something very innocent, or he might be in some kind of terrible fix. And as well as wanting to avoid government programs and entanglements that would only slow him down, he suddenly didn't want to see this kind and eager woman get into trouble.

He made his tone curt, designed to wound. "My business is my own, lady. Keep your nose out of it."

Conscience pierced him as her wide, beautiful green eyes grew luminous. She blinked once, then amazingly, opened her mouth to argue.

"We're at the city limits now," he growled, cutting her off and yanking away his seat belt. "Let me out here."

Karen shut her mouth, grimaced, but found she couldn't disobey the force of Judd's command. She pulled into the parking lot of the Creekside Diner and stopped.

"Thanks for the lift." He didn't *sound* the least bit thankful as he opened the car door.

"Why don't you let me buy you something to eat." She reached out to touch his sleeve. "You must be hungry."

"No." He shrugged her hand off like a gnat and climbed out.

"What's wrong? Did I say something to offend you?"

He pivoted impatiently, the door between them. "No, of course not."

She suddenly wanted to cry in frustration. She had rushed into this assignment with misplaced confidence, and now she was making a hash of it. For a few minutes, she'd thought they were establishing a rapport, and now he couldn't wait to get away from her. Nothing in her training had prepared her for this. She'd never felt so incredibly off balance as she had since picking up Judd Maxwell. And if she let him go now, she'd never know if he became reunited with his family, or wound up on the streets, or what had happened to him!

"Let me at least buy you an iced tea or a soft drink or something," she said, grasping at straws, no longer trying to hide her desperation. "You'll get dehydrated walking in this heat, otherwise, and it won't take long."

Maxwell scowled. She couldn't tell if he was annoyed, or shamed that he'd brought her close to tears, or both. But as he reluctantly nodded assent, it didn't matter.

She beamed, and he held up a warning palm. "Just one drink, then I'll have to be on my way. I've got important business in Silver Creek." '

KAREN HAD NEVER DINED with a wooden Indian before, but she guessed there was a first time for everything.

It was blissfully cool in the air-conditioned restaurant. Though it was located on the edge of town, good cooking made the diner a popular spot with locals, and many of the seats were taken. At their window-side table, well-worn but clean venetian blinds kept the glare from Karen's eyes. A fly, buzzing against the glass, was exhibiting more personality than her companion.

His pronouncement that he "had business" in Silver Creek had astounded her, and she'd blurted out a hopeful "Is your memory returning?"

She'd gotten nothing for her hopefulness but a curt "No." And guessing at the pain that might underlie the surliness, she hadn't pressed him further. He had, more than likely, made up the business line as an excuse to get away from her as soon as they finished their drink.

But much as she wanted to be understanding, she was getting tired of Judd Maxwell sitting across from her behind his shades, ignoring the menu, obviously determined to ignore her also. She wondered if he'd eaten anything since lunch. He had walked about eight miles from the center of Granite to where she picked him up. After a long hike in the heat, he had to be famished.

She sat forward and casually offered to buy him dinner, but he proved, not surprisingly, stubborn. There was one tactic that had worked on him before, maybe she should try it again.

"Please, I'm really hungry," she fibbed. "I'll be too embarrassed to eat by myself if you don't order something."

Maxwell expelled his breath in a long gust, jerked off his glasses and picked up the plastic-covered menu.

She noted his eyes were steel gray, complementing the austere planes of his bearded face. She frowned to herself; to find a harder man, she'd need a police lineup.

She started to lift her own menu, then realized his expression was changing. His dark brows bunched together, forming lines on his forehead, and he swallowed.

"Anything wrong?" she asked.

He cleared his throat. "Not really."

Curious, she watched him impatiently scan the bill of fare. Wasn't this coffee shop good enough for him? What was he used to, nouvelle cuisine? Her patience with him had reached its limit.

"There's a lot there," she said, "surely you see *something* you like."

He cleared his throat again, then squeezed his forehead between thumb and index finger in a gesture of exasperation. When he looked up, there was a startling uncertainty in his eyes. "What are you having?"

Karen caught her breath. It was the menu. He couldn't make sense of it. *He couldn't remember.*

A lump formed in her throat. "Um, I'll have a hamburger. I think you'd like them." She smiled for him. "Besides, *anything* you order here has got to be better than hospital food."

He shifted in his seat. "I can picture clearly everything on the page," he assured her, then added more softly, "I'm just having some difficulty remembering what I like."

When their plates came, Karen let him eat in peace. She wanted to ask him what business he claimed to have in Silver Creek, and a few other things, but she decided it would be best to let him enjoy his meal. He had excellent table manners and didn't scarf like a pig, but he didn't waste a bite, either. She'd been right that he was hungry.

When she looked up later, she caught Judd Maxwell watching her. He'd finished his burger and was leaning back in the chair, quite obviously assessing her. His eyes were narrowed and had deepened from battleship gray to something darker and sexier. They traveled slowly up from her hands, which rested on the table's edge, to her forearms, to her breasts beneath the green silk blouse....

She felt her nipples harden, and quickly shifted her gaze to the salt and pepper shakers, hoping she didn't look as flushed as she felt. There was no denying she was turned on by him—he exuded masculinity. But why *he* was responding to *her* this way confused her. The men she dated enjoyed her ready sense of humor, and she realized that with her stable, giving nature she was often taken for granted. But she couldn't remember once receiving an appreciative stare like this one. Since she was a youngster, she'd been referred to politely as a "big girl" and, except for her proportionately large bosom and the rich auburn of her curly hair, men had never given her much of a second look.

When she dared to glance at him again, Maxwell had closed his eyes. It was a rare moment of repose; the sharpness had gone, and beneath the bad-boy slickness of his mahogany hair, his features were strong and handsome. His beard was a shade lighter than his hair, growing out fast to cover his upper lip and jaw but shaved clean around his neck. She loved beards but had never felt one. Were the short, curling hairs wiry or silky? She wished she could reach out and touch. And now, though Vivian and she had only joked about it, she really wished she knew if he was married.

"Can I get you anything else?" the waitress asked.

"No, ah, I think we're done," Karen mumbled. "Do you want anything else, Judd?" It was the first time she'd called him by his first name. It made her feel oddly self-conscious.

He shook his head no.

The gangly waitress looked about eighteen. Her blond ponytail swung as she turned to Judd. "I haven't seen you in here in a while, Judd," she said. "Been busy at the station?"

Judd shot forward in his chair, jarring the table and sloshing his water glass. "You know me?"

The girl looked down, startled at the intent gaze that bored through her. "'Course. I've waited on you once or twice, don't you remember?"

"When?"

She shrugged. "I don't know. I've only been here four months. Why are you looking at me so strange?" She took a step back.

"I'm sorry." Judd shook his head in apology. "You mentioned a station?"

"Yeah, the Chevron station uptown. I thought you worked there."

Maxwell glanced at Karen. There were two Chevrons in Silver Creek; Karen never frequented the one on North Main, because it was out of her way, but she knew exactly where it was. She nodded at Judd.

"Thanks for asking," he said in a normal voice. "Things are fine at the station. I'm sorry, I forgot your name."

"It's Allison. That's okay, a person can't remember everything."

Karen wanted to smile. In Maxwell's case, Allison didn't realize what an understatement that was.

"Hey, Allie, get a move on." A middle-aged waitress in a tank top passed by, her arms filled with plates. "With Mar on vacation, you've got no time for lollygagging."

"Sorry," the girl murmured.

Then Karen noticed the cook. The burly, moon-faced man had come out from the kitchen to draw himself a soft drink and was staring at Allison and Judd. Karen understood the annoyance of the overworked waitress, but the cook was positively glaring.

KAREN COULD FEEL the excitement crackling out of Judd Maxwell, and she shared it. The fact he worked in Silver Creek meant they could get him back home today. Being in familiar surroundings was sure to bring his memory back!

He still didn't seem anxious to talk, but he'd made no argument this time about accepting a lift from her to the gas station where he worked. If they had to stop at one more red light as they crossed town, she wouldn't put it past him to jump out and run.

"Do you recognize anything?" she asked.

He gave a negative grunt in response, and Karen felt a fresh wave of compassion for him. How strange and frightening it would be to look around Silver Creek and not recognize anything. She concentrated on the storefronts as they passed, trying to see them through unfamiliar eyes. The shoe store with its pre-season display of snow boots. The drugstore, whose orange-and-black sign had overhung the sidewalk

ever since she was a baby. Garibaldi's Grocery with
the weekly specials written on butcher paper, taped
to the window. She sometimes tired of spending her
life in the same small town that revolved around mining and logging and that derived its excitement from
the fishing, hunting and skiing, depending on the sea-
son. But now she was suddenly very glad for the
predictability of Silver Creek. It was comforting
knowing these streets like her own name, especially
since her mother had passed away.

"Judd," she said, "what did you mean, before
dinner, when you said you had business here? Were
you just trying to get rid of me?"

"No. The highway patrol impounded my car. It's
in their yard here."

"Oh." Ironic. She'd just been assuring herself
how well she knew Silver Creek, yet she'd never
realized they kept towed cars at the HP station. She
thought a moment about that other thing that had
puzzled her. "I was told that, when they picked you
up, you'd been robbed. How did you get your hair
cut this afternoon if you left the hospital without any
money?"

"On my way out, one of the nurses insisted on
giving me a twenty."

"Hmm." Was any female immune to the man's
hotheaded charm? It seemed not. She wondered why
he'd chosen to spend his money at the barber's; together with the sunglasses he wore, it seemed almost
like a disguise. "If you don't mind my asking, why
did you get your hair cut?"

He shrugged. "It was driving me crazy that long.
How far is it to the station?"

She had to smile at the eagerness in his voice. "Just a few more blocks."

It was encouraging to see him excited in a positive way rather than tense. He'd certainly been uptight before the waitress recognized him. Karen had noticed the way he unobtrusively scanned the diner when they first entered. He was doubtless simply trying to remember the place, but she'd gotten the weird feeling for a moment he was sweeping the room for foes.

"That must be it," Judd said, pointing to the Summers' Chevron sign a block ahead.

"Yes. Does it look familiar?" When he didn't respond, she was disappointed. "Want me to wait for you?"

He seemed to withdraw into himself once more. "Thanks, but you've already done more than enough for me."

"I was glad to do it."

Karen pulled into the station, and Judd jumped out. Two repair bays stood open, but the only attendant had his back to them as he saw a customer off at the pumps.

Karen parked the Festiva next to a phone booth and headed for the ladies' room inside the office. She watched from the corner of her eye as Judd tapped the attendant on the shoulder of his blue coveralls. He was a short man, not reaching Judd's chin.

"Excuse me, are you Mr. Summers?"

"Yeah, I'm Howie Summers." The fortyish man turned, screwed up his ill-shaven face and spit tobacco juice between his feet and Judd's. "Very funny, Maxwell. So, you're back, huh? I knew you'd regret giving me the brush-off, but I brought my

nephew in. He needs a job, and he's no ingrate like
you, so you can get lost.''

Karen stood frozen, watching. Judd's jaw
clenched. He was obviously lost for a response to the
sudden tirade, but he didn't back off. ''I need to ask
you a few questions.''

''Well, if it's about your pay, you ain't got no
more comin'.'' The bantam punctuated his words
with a jabbing finger. ''You might as well get back
in the car with your floozy and take off.''

Judd swiveled, saw Karen, then closed the gap between himself and Summers. He whipped off his
glasses. ''I don't know what your beef is with me,
Summers, but you'd better apologize to the young
lady, or I'll shove your teeth down your throat.''

The other man stepped back. Karen thought his
sandy hair might stand on end. His head jerked toward her, but he wouldn't meet her eye. ''I apologize, miss, no offense meant. Your friend and I ain't
on the best of terms and I, ah, wasn't thinking what
I was sayin'.''

A sports car and a motor home pulled into the
station, both heading for the full-serve pumps. ''We
need to talk,'' Judd said, ''but I'll come back later,
when you're not busy. For now, just tell me where I
live.''

''Tell you where you live?''

''Yes. The street address.''

Summers licked his lips. ''Ah, 200 Meadow, I
think. Yeah, 200.''

Judd took Karen's elbow. ''You know where
Meadow is?'' he asked Karen in a quiet voice.

''Sure.''

When they were back in the car, Karen hesitated

to mention the scene, but it felt equally awkward pretending it hadn't happened. "What was that all about?"

"I don't know. I'll find out later, when he's cooled down."

"It sounds like you two had a knock-down-drag-out. Do you think it had anything to do with you losing your memory?"

"I don't know," he repeated, "but somehow I can't imagine feeling too cut up over an argument with a jerk like Summers."

Karen giggled, but she felt bad for Judd just the same. What rotten luck! Though Summers had probably pushed him to the limit of his endurance, this was no time for Judd to be worrying about finding a new job. She hoped he had some savings to fall back on and made a mental note to start looking for employment for him tomorrow.

The apartment building was only three blocks away. She vaguely remembered that at one time it had been a motel, but the neon sign on the front lawn was gone.

Karen pulled in the driveway of the horseshoe-shaped building while Judd twisted in his seat to extricate a key ring. "It must be number 8," he said, reading the number off one of the keys. Karen parked in the space across from the unit.

It was her job to take a look at his apartment, assess if it was a safe place for a man in his condition to recuperate. Deciding it might be wiser *not* to ask his permission, she simply followed him as he exited the car. To her relief, he seemed too preoccupied to care.

Judd's neighbors had their door open, and Karen

glanced briefly their way, then waited while Judd worked the key. Criminy, it was hot out here. The setting sun was directly behind them. She was sure if she perspired much more, her new silk blouse would be ruined.

Judd pushed the apartment door open. From inside came a tremendous scream.

Chapter Three

Karen skittered backward over the edge of the sidewalk and lost her balance for a sickening moment before Judd grabbed her arm. He steadied her, then quickly drew off his dark glasses and stepped into the apartment.

Karen waited outside a few moments. Scared, but worried for Judd's safety, she cautiously moved to the threshold and peered inside. The apartment was very dark, and the air was more fetid than simply stale, like the smell of something decomposing. She fought the urge to gag as she clamped a hand over her nose and mouth.

When her eyes adjusted to the dim light, she located Judd near the center of the room. He was bent at the waist, looking into a large, ornate cage against the wall. A fresh cry issued from behind the bars.

"It's just a bird?" she asked with chagrin. She joined him. "It's a...cockatiel, isn't it?"

"Yes, and very hungry from the sound of it."

The gray-and-white bird stretched up toward them on tiptoe, its yellow crest erect as it gave a series of loud whistles and caws.

Judd straightened. "Where's his food?"

Karen pulled a coffee can off the entertainment center next to the cage. "Is this it?" She peeled the top off; rather than seed, it was filled with sandy-colored granules.

"Here." He impatiently took the can from her and withdrew a coffee measuring spoon.

"I've never heard of feeding a bird anything like *that*."

His arm was in the cage, removing the plastic food cup. "Well, we've got to give the little troublemaker *something* to shut him up."

"Troublemaker!" the cockatiel crowed.

Karen's mouth fell open.

The parrot danced on its perch as Judd replaced the food cup. "Troublemaker. Troublemaker. Howdy-do?"

Karen laughed, allowing her astonishment to spill out. Her delight seemed infectious, because a crooked smile, the first she'd seen, appeared on Judd's face.

"I'd say you two have met before," she said.

"Yeah, the bird's a good judge of character," he said, wiping his hands on his jeans. Though the words were self-mocking, she could tell he was amused.

"Oh, my." She wiped a tear from her eye as she watched the parrot tuck into its food. "I didn't know cockatiels could talk. He's so cute. What's his name?"

The mask dropped back over his face. "I've no idea." He brushed past her, into the kitchen alcove. She bit her lip, knowing it would do no good to apologize for her thoughtless question.

Through the pass-through, she watched him open

several cupboards before finding a stack of foam cups. "Let's get some light in here," she said.

Judd exited the kitchen as she was opening the front drape. "There's only beer and tap water and no ice, but help yourself," he said. "I can't believe how hot it is in here!" He crouched before the air conditioner and began examining the controls.

As Karen surveyed the studio apartment, she realized the blond-wood and vinyl upholstered furnishings were similar to the ones she'd glimpsed next door; apparently Judd had rented the place furnished. Pushed out of the way between the front door and an entertainment center was a black weightlifter's bench with several pairs of hefty dumbbells lined up beneath it. A single bed sat flush against the back wall, a cream-colored comforter hastily pulled up to the headboard. She casually noted he must be unattached, after all. She told herself this was unfortunate, that Judd might have no one to help him through his recovery but herself, but she couldn't quite feel genuinely sorry. She hiked her purse higher on her shoulder and decided to slip into the bathroom while Judd was busy.

Bracing herself for the moldy odors of the typical bachelor bathroom, she was pleasantly surprised to find Judd's clean and smelling of soap and good aftershave.

The only sign of disarray was a pair of burgundy leather slippers kicked into the corner. A navy robe, pegged to the back of the door, brushed her hand as she moved into the room. The rich fabric felt like silk, piped in contrasting satin to match the color of the slippers.

The bathroom fixtures looked about twenty years

old, the yellowed linoleum due for replacement, but the handsome navy plaid towels carefully hung on the rack were huge and plushy. A tag peeped out: Polo, by Ralph Lauren.

His toothbrush in the porcelain holder was another surprise. Staring at it while she washed her hands, Karen realized that, like expensive hairbrushes, it was fashioned of wood and natural animal bristles. Karen shook her head; people were endlessly surprising and contradictory. Judd's personal possessions seemed more appropriate for a gentleman with a valet than for a small-town gas jockey.

When she came out, the air conditioner was softly humming and Judd was leafing through his clothes closet.

"You've got a nice place here," she said.

Judd glanced over his shoulder, blank eyes scanned the room, and he grunted. With a stab of compassion, she understood how he must feel, standing in the midst of a space that should have been very personal to him, yet was totally unfamiliar. She could understand why Judd looked so troubled, so intent, as he examined his belongings.

Feeling suddenly self-conscious, Karen shifted her gaze to the small stack of magazines on the coffee table, picked one up and glanced through it. It was full of technical articles on stereo equipment and reviews of new recordings. A pair of highly polished mahogany speakers stood on ebony stands at either end of the entertainment center, and a complicated looking compact disc player and tuner sat on one of the open shelves. There was a shoe box of CDs beside it. He had eclectic taste: opera, jazz, groups with strange names she'd never heard of. And there were a few of her own favorites: Barbra Streisand, Sting, Annie Lennox.

Judd approached but didn't reprimand her for her snooping, simply pulled down the door of the entertainment center's built-in desk.

"Are you looking for anything specific?" she asked.

"An address book."

"Oh. Want me to help you?"

When he didn't answer, she decided to take it for a yes, and started with the small number of books in front of her on the shelf. "Car manuals, hardcover best-sellers. No address book. Handsome bookends, though."

She passed into the tiny kitchen with its ancient refrigerator and gas stove. There was no phone, but checking the cabinets for the address book would be a good excuse to make sure he had enough groceries.

The first cupboard contained a package of paper plates and cups—no real dishes in sight. In the silverware drawer, she found plastic utensils. It was a perfect opportunity to try cheering him up with a little humor.

"I can tell you one thing," she called.

For a second, she thought he wasn't going to respond, then he said, "What's that?"

"You've got a phobia for sudsy water."

"What?" It didn't take him a moment. "Oh, the paper plates. Well, no one likes dishpan hands."

Karen smiled, pleased he'd responded in kind.

A well-thumbed *Joy of Cooking* sat next to containers of pepper and salt, a few cereal boxes, canned goods and dried pasta. The rest of the overhead cupboards were empty. "You're no Julia Child," she observed.

"Yeah? Well, I'm probably a demon with a can opener."

Inspecting the cupboard next to the stove, she almost whistled. "Hey, I take that back, you may be a gourmet after all." An expensive set of French stainless steel skillets and saucepans gleamed out at her. In the cupboard beside it was a Krups espresso maker.

Checking the refrigerator last, she found only a frozen package of New York steaks, three bottles of imported beer and half a loaf of sliced french bread. Karen bit her lip. It might take some time to find him a new job, and he'd obviously need groceries before then.

"I don't think you do much entertaining," she called, "or else it's B.Y.O.E.—Bring Your Own Everything."

"Maybe that's why no address book, I don't have any friends."

That brought her to the doorway; he was back at the desk, staring morosely at its wood grain surface.

"Perhaps you didn't need a book because you have a great memory for numbers. I know that sounds facetious, but what I mean is, it could very well be true. And you're sure to get your memory back—you just have to give it time."

"It won't be a moment too soon for me!" Judd threw down a stack of junk mail. "This doesn't seem to be getting me anywhere. I've got thirty years of a life behind me, why can't I remember any of it!"

She moved to stand next to him. "I know. It can't be easy." She thought he might tell her she couldn't possibly know how difficult it was and to leave him alone, but he didn't, just leaned forward on his knuckles, his head turned so she could no longer see the black frustration in his face.

After a few quiet moments, she said, "You didn't find anything helpful in the desk?"

"No. No records, no checkbook, no paid bills. Either I just moved here or I paid my bills in cash or my checkbook was stolen from the car when the thieves took my wallet." He tossed the mail back into the desk. "I was hoping a phone bill might show frequently called numbers."

"A lot of people don't keep their bill stubs. Once you get some ID, the phone company may be able to give you back copies."

Judd grunted agreement. "I'll try to locate my landlord tonight and ask him if I gave any references when I rented this place."

His face preoccupied, Judd moved to the birdcage. Noting his approach, the cockatiel abandoned its food and crawled onto the perch nearest the wrought-iron door.

"I think he wants to come out," Karen said.

Judd unlatched the door and extended his index finger; the bird climbed on. Karen watched as Judd began massaging his pet's neck between thumb and forefinger. The vigor with which he rubbed looked hard enough to wring the bird's slender neck, alarming Karen, but the cockatiel's eyelids slowly closed in an expression of what seemed sheer contentment.

Judd realized what he was doing and snorted softly. "Strange, I don't remember this little guy at all, yet I seem to know how to handle him."

"I see that. It must be like riding a bicycle—physical acts are things you never forget how to do." Her own words formed a question in her mind of what other physical acts this virile stranger might instinctively remember. She blushed, and was glad when he didn't look at her or seem to catch the double meaning.

As she watched, she became mesmerized by the rhythmic stroking of Judd's fingers through the bird's soft gray feathers. His tanned hands were large, the fingers blunt-tipped but not at all coarse. She pictured the wide, warm palms deeply kneading her own shoulders...the strong thumbs deftly easing the tension from her neck...one hand moving to her face to trace a lingering line along her jaw.

"That's enough," Judd said.

Karen's dreamily narrowed eyes snapped open as Judd kissed the bird's head and returned it to its cage. She coughed. A warmth that had nothing to do with the outside temperature was simmering inside her; she shifted her weight to the other foot to squelch the erotic sensation.

Judd crossed one arm over his chest and with the other hand squeezed his forehead.

"Are you remembering something?"

"No, darn it. I get this feeling every once in a while. It's like there's a...a bubble in my head. It expands, and I'm sure it's about to burst and I'll remember something, and then it just recedes and disappears. I had the same premonition when we first walked into the apartment, and again just now, but nothing came of it. One thing I *am* almost sure of, some item, an important one, is missing."

Karen glanced about. "There's no sign you had a

burglar while you were in the hospital. Could it just be part of an overall apprehension you feel, caused by the amnesia?''

"No," he said decisively, "it's not that." He paced the length of the room, slicing with his hand. "Some *thing* that should be here is missing. And I've got a feeling if I only knew what it was, everything else would come back."

IT'S JUST ANOTHER *Wednesday morning,* Karen told herself, *so why do I feel, so…different?*

She set the plate of cat food on the paper next to the refrigerator, gave her cat, Toby, a stroke, then poured her first cup of coffee. Yesterday she'd wondered how it must be for Judd to see familiar places through strange eyes; now she felt a bit as if she knew. She carried her cup out to the living room and tucked her legs under her on the sofa. Staring out at the back garden through the sunporch, she reflected that everything looked just a little different since her completely out of the ordinary experience of the day before.

She'd lain awake a long time last night, thinking of ways to get Judd back into a psychiatrist's office, pondering how she could help him locate friends and family who might help bring his memory back.

She always enjoyed mapping out strategies to aid her clients, but last night she'd been charged with an unusual exhilaration, and her thoughts about Judd Maxwell had threatened to veer from the strictly professional. Knowing so little about him, and faced with the possibility that he might have a wife or lover somewhere, she had restrained herself from picturing him in any kind of romantic context. But just barely.

Karen had thought that in the sobering light of a
new day her client would seem less fascinating, but
the enigma he presented continued to intrigue her.
Though he obviously had a taste for the finer things
in life, he'd chosen to rent an apartment with fake
wood furnishings. Why? Had he grown up in a rich
family, or worked as a lawyer or in some other high-
paying profession before suffering a reversal of fortune?

Karen reminded herself she'd better eat some
breakfast, and got up with a sigh to fix it. Such fan-
ciful possibilities about Judd's life were fun to consider, but not realistic. The answer had to be much
more mundane. He probably had champagne tastes
and a beer budget, and when he could afford it, he
bought a luxury item here and there.

Still, as she ate her cereal at the dining table, she
decided she had not imagined his compelling masculine aura. Unbidden, her mind kept conjuring up a
picture of him, white shirt spread taut against the
muscles of his back as he bent over his dresser. Then
the thrust of his hip as he rested his weight on one
leg, his bronze arms braced like pillars on the desk-
top. The suggestive gleam in his pewter eyes as he
studied her in the diner—*that* she would *not* let herself remember. The episode had not been repeated
after dinner, and she'd probably read more interest
into the look than truly existed on Judd's part. Remembering it brought a guilty flush of desire to her
cheeks, and it was best forgotten if she and the troubled man were to work together to get him back on
his feet.

She checked the wall clock— seven-thirty. He was
probably up by now. She glanced at the phone. No,

calling to arrange her next appointment with him wasn't a good idea. She didn't want him to race to the ringing telephone, hoping it was his mother or best friend or someone who could tell him about his past, only to find it was that social worker woman, the one who was so sure she was being helpful and really only getting in his way.

It was clear that the thornily independent man had warmed somewhat toward her yesterday, but he still wasn't ready to acknowledge he needed her assistance. Well, he needed to pick up his car, and the impound yard was several miles from his apartment. Her only appointment in Granite City wasn't until this afternoon, so she had plenty of time. If she casually dropped by and offered Judd a ride, it would be the perfect excuse to talk to him. She'd better hurry, though, or he might strike out on his own. Forgoing a second cup of coffee, Karen headed for her bedroom to dress.

She was on her way out to the car when a big blue Mercedes pulled up to the curb and a woman in a brightly colored caftan popped out. Karen groaned. She was always happy to see her landlady and friend, Mrs. Cohen. Except when she was in a rush.

"Hello, dear," the heavyset, fiftyish woman called. "I was driving by and wanted to tell you I'm going to bring Truman by tomorrow, to help us with the color scheme for the new paint job. How are you this morning?"

"Fine, Mrs. Cohen." Karen noted she was wearing the flaming orange wig this morning. "I'm off to an appointment with a client."

"In town?"

"Yes." Because she lived in the northern end of

Granite County, Karen was often assigned clients in the Silver Creek area.

"How interesting. It's not old Morris, is it? He's been doddering around the last five years, Lord love him."

Mrs. Cohen always spoke with volume; from twenty paces she was shouting. Karen reluctantly came down the driveway to set her gossipy friend straight. "No, it's not Mr. Morris, nothing like that."

Mrs. Cohen raised her eyebrows. "A younger man, then? Are you sure you're meeting a client? You're looking particularly fetching this morning, my dear. And I must confess, I saw you driving through town with a young fellow yesterday, though I wasn't close enough to see who it was."

Karen tugged at her above-knee skirt. "I'm sorry, Mrs. Cohen, I really can't discuss my cases."

Mrs. Cohen patted her arm. "You shouldn't be embarrassed about your boyfriends, Karen—every woman needs a life apart from her work. I'm sure your own mother, God rest her soul, would say the same thing. If you're always thinking about the needs of others, your own life will pass you by." She beetled her brows, which were an incongruous black beneath the fiery wig. "You know I'd never tell you what to do, Karen, but since I'm admonishing you to have a good time, the only thing I *wouldn't* recommend is sleeping with some man before you're married."

Karen blinked. She'd received her friend's favorite motherly lecture more than once, always unnecessarily, but this morning it caught her by surprise. "You don't have to worry, Mrs. Cohen. I have neither the inclination nor the opportunity for such a thing.''

''Don't worry about the opportunity, Karen. You can't attract a man without eliciting propositions. Most of them are always ready for it, whether you are or not.'' She clucked knowingly at the younger woman, ''Remember, it's your *own* inclination that can get you in trouble.''

Karen remembered Judd stroking his cockatiel's feathers, and the absurdly sexual way she'd reacted to the innocent performance. Yesterday she would have laughed at Mrs. Cohen's warning, but today...?

By the time she reached the door of Judd Maxwell's apartment, Karen had convinced herself she had her emotions under control, and there was no reason to feel awkward with him.

Then Judd answered the door dressed only in worn jeans that barely clung to his hips.

Karen nearly dropped to the pavement. From his tousled hair to his bare feet, he looked disheveled, and sexy as the devil. Karen coughed and kept her gaze on his face. His eyes above the brown beard were tired but not bloodshot, so he probably wasn't hungover, just hadn't slept much.

He inhaled loudly, and his zombielike expression metamorphosed into disapproval. ''I should have known it was you.'' He leaned one bare arm up along the door frame. ''You must be crazy, spending all your time running after a psycho like me, or are you just nosey?''

The words stung, but she'd prepared herself this time for his initial rejection. She scowled fiercely and set her hands on her hips. ''You've forgotten your manners, along with your past life, Maxwell.'' Illustrating her point, she looked his naked chest up and down with an expression of disgust.

Masses of dark hair swirled around his abdomen. The hairs fanned up and across his flat stomach and over the slightly rounded and hard muscles of his chest. More fine hair tufted beneath the junction of his muscular arm and molded shoulder. A tightening in her belly almost wiped the mock frown from her face, but she kept it pasted on.

Judd's expression was less belligerent as her eyes returned to his.

In a more reasonable tone of voice, he said, "If you knew what kind of night I had, I don't think you'd be beating down my door."

"Don't worry. I'm tougher than I look."

Judd's lips quirked in something like approval. "I believe that." He paused a beat, seemed to be considering something. "I'm sorry." He stood up straight. "When you knocked, I was still in bed." He reached out tentatively and lightly touched her cheek.

Karen gasped.

He ran his fingers down to her chin. "I'm not usually rude to lovely women," he said wistfully. His lids lowered as his gaze held hers, his lashes long and dusky.

When his hand slowly dropped back to his side, Karen felt disconcerted. She swallowed. His touch was so tender, his gaze almost longing, contradicting the harshness of the words he had spoken a moment before.

Judd stepped back and opened the door wide. As he allowed her to pass, he cursed himself, both for upsetting her and for letting her talk her way into his apartment again. He waved her toward a chair and mumbled something about would she wait a minute, then went to dress.

Since leaving the hospital, he'd had the chilling feeling he was being pursued, or at least being watched. In an effort to alter his appearance, he'd had his hair restyled and refused the barber's offer to shave his rapidly growing beard. When Karen drove him to his apartment, he'd more than half expected to find either a detective or a thug lying in wait for him. He couldn't tell which.

Late into the night, he'd lain awake, trying with all his might to bring his fears into focus, to remember the source of them and recall exactly what kind of danger he was in. But the apprehension, though strong, remained nebulous. His greatest fear was that on meeting his enemy he would fail to recognize the man, giving the other a deadly advantage. And if his premonitions were more than dark fantasy, he didn't want Karen Thomas anywhere near when the confrontation came.

Karen sat at the dinette table while Judd dressed in the bathroom. The cockatiel preened in its cage as Karen's pulse slowly returned to normal. The effect her client's touch had had on her was powerful and disconcerting, and she carefully kept her eyes averted from his rumpled bed. Being secretly attracted to Judd was one thing; having him respond as he had in her fantasies was another! Things were clearly getting out of hand.

While she waited, she had a stern, reassuring talk with herself. When Judd reappeared, she refused to feel any sense of pleasure that he'd shaved his neck but left the becoming beard and mustache. And the fact he was wearing stiff new jeans and a crisp white polo shirt surely didn't mean he wanted to impress her.

"I came by to give you a ride to the highway patrol to pick up your car," she explained.

Judd frowned as he pulled his work boots out from under the bed and sat down in a vinyl easy chair to put them on. "Thanks," he said, "but I don't want to keep you from your other clients." His demeanor was firm, polite, detached.

So, apparently he, too, had thought better of getting too close. She shut away the whisper of disappointment and told herself this was progress. "It's no trouble." Seeing he was about to refuse her offer, she added, "I've got an awfully light caseload this week, and if I don't put in some time with you, my boss is going to think I've been goofing off."

She crossed her fingers hoping he would weaken, but he still looked remote and disinterested. Then the phone rang.

As the peal rent the air, Judd's eyes flew to hers and they shared an electrifying moment of suspense and fear shot through with hope. Then he was out of his chair and in two long strides grabbed the phone off the kitchen wall behind her.

"Hello."

Karen clasped her hands tight in her lap.

"This is Maxwell.... Yes." Judd's voice came down an octave in disappointment. "I see.... I'm leaving now. I'll be there in a few minutes."

He didn't make her wait or ask who it was. "That was Howie Summers," he said almost apologetically. "There's an automotive computer down at the shop he can't figure out. He wants me to stop by and see if I can get it working.''

Karen sighed, then forced a smile. ''We can stop by there on the way to get your car.''

At least the disappointment of the call had distracted him from refusing her ride.

As they drove out of the complex in Karen's car, she started down the mental list of things she needed to discuss with him. ''Did you get to talk to the apartment manager last night?''

''No, he was out all evening. I spent a few minutes chatting with one of my neighbors, but apparently he only knew me by sight.''

''I was talking with someone from the hospital last night,'' Karen said carefully. Vivian had called her right after she got home, and they'd discussed Judd for some time. ''They say that dreams can be a window of the subconscious. Do you remember anything you dreamed last night?''

Judd turned his face to the window. ''No.''

''Nothing at all?''

''I said no!'' Then, almost immediately, ''I'm sorry. I warned you I got up on the wrong side of the bed.''

She returned his weak smile, but she wondered. He slid his eyes away, and for the first time, Karen had the distinct feeling Judd Maxwell wasn't telling her the truth.

Chapter Four

Karen waited in the car while Judd went into the station to find his former employer.

She fidgeted in her seat. She didn't want to crowd her client; given Judd's vulnerable position, she felt he needed her to engender self-confidence, not smother him. But she couldn't help wishing she was a fly on the wall in the station. She almost expected the two men to stumble out the door, locked in a fistfight, because of the way they'd bristled at one another last evening. But several minutes passed, and there were no shouts or curses from within.

A car pulled in, and a skinny young man emerged from the office to man the full-service pump. It was undoubtedly Summers' nephew, Karen thought, the one he'd hired in Judd's place. The boy looked bored, and didn't make eye contact with his customer. Karen thought of the favor Judd was doing this very moment for his ex-employer, and wondered if Summers might be persuaded to give Judd his job back. Perhaps, as Judd's social worker, she could help facilitate that, if she got a chance.

After a quarter of an hour, she decided it would be natural and acceptable to check on Judd. She eased out of the car, made sure her dress was straight, and avoided sticking her high heels in the oily patches on the blacktop.

She found the men in the back of the shop, their heads together as they studied an LCD readout on a piece of machinery. "I see," Howie was saying. "Yeah, I think I got it now."

Karen cleared her throat. "Excuse me, are you about finished, Judd?" As the two men looked up, she suddenly remembered how Howie Summers had referred to her as a floozy the day before.

"Yes, I think we're finished here," Judd said. "Summers, this is a friend of mine, Karen Thomas."

Howie fell in with him, nodding politely to Karen as though he'd never seen her before. Well, Karen thought, if Summers was going to be on his good behavior, maybe now was the time to see if he could help her client. If she knew anything about male pride, Judd probably needed her to break the ice.

"How do you do, Mr. Summers." She pulled one of her business cards from her purse and handed it to him. "Mr. Maxwell and I are just on our way to pick up his car at the highway-patrol office. Has Judd had time to tell you about his unfortunate accident last Friday night?"

Howie was staring in bemusement at her card. "Accident?" He glanced up at the taller man, who sent a darted glance at Karen. "No, Judd, ah, didn't mention any accident."

Karen raised her eyebrows a fraction at Judd, offering him a chance to jump in. He cleared his throat, then gave Howie a sketchy summary of how he'd been picked up by the highway patrol following an apparent robbery and was having trouble remembering the details. Karen noticed he didn't use the *a* word, but Howie did it for him.

"You mean you got amnesia? Gosh a'mighty, I can't believe it. Why didn't you say so?" He stared at Judd in open wonder. "Does that mean you don't remember our fight, or nothin'? Golly, I thought something was wrong, with you actin' so funny last night. I couldn't figure you out, calling me 'Mr. Summers' and all. I thought you were making fun of me or something."

"No, not at all," Karen said. "So perhaps now that you understand Judd has had some setbacks, you might let bygones be bygones and rehire him?"

Summers' shoulders twitched and his face turned red. "Oh, yeah, sure, I would. It's just, well, I only need one guy, and I promised my sister I'd give her boy the job. He's nineteen, he needs somethin' to do to keep him outta trouble. You know what I mean. He's nowhere near as handy as you, Judd, he's just starting out, but my sister wants him to learn a trade. I promised her, and I can't afford two mechanics. You understand."

"That's all right," Judd said, his posture wooden. "Don't trouble yourself. I'm sure I can find work elsewhere."

"Yeah, yeah. You were only part-time, anyway, and there's a lot of garages in town might need a good mechanic. Hey, I'll give you a reference, okay?"

"Fine." Judd half turned, laid the manual he'd been holding on the tool bench. "While we're here, you might as well tell me what happened Friday night. It might help."

"Sure thing, let me think." Howie rubbed a grimy

knuckle along his forehead. "You left work at five, same as usual. Then you came back later, couple hours later, it must have been about seven. Yeah, I'm sure it was 'cause the baseball game was just about to start on the radio and you kind of interrupted."

"Why did I come back?"

"You wanted your pay. You always get paid the last day of the month, but you were all hot and bothered this time, wanted me to pay what I owed you for the first two weeks of the month, 'stead of waiting. Well, my bookkeeping's not set up to do that, and naturally, I said no. Then you got steamed, said I owed it to you. I didn't like it, and I told you I'd give you the dough, but if you took it, you should never come back. I guess, in the back of my mind, I'm thinking about my sister and my nephew, you know."

Judd nodded.

"So, did you give him the money?" Karen asked.

"Yeah. I figured it out rough, 'cause he wanted it right then, in cash, and I got it out of the drawer. Then he took off in his car, and that's the last I saw of him."

"And that was about seven-fifteen, would you say?" Judd asked.

"Yeah, about that."

Further questioning on Judd's part elicited the few facts Howie Summers knew about his employee. Judd had moved to Silver Creek only two or three months ago, had once lived in Los Angeles and, Howie was fairly certain, was divorced. Howie had hired Judd on the strength of a successful pop quiz on car repairs and an impressive first day's performance on the job. Since he never bothered to ask for a résumé or job application, he had no idea where Judd had worked before. As well as fixing cars, Judd had seemed to know a lot about older vehicles and collectible cars.

"SO YOU WERE ABLE to fix Howie's computer problem?" Karen asked when they were back in the Festiva.

"Yeah. All it took was reading the manual. The nephew was trying to help him when I arrived, but he wasn't listening."

"Working for a relative can be difficult. If the boy doesn't stay, you could approach Howie again about getting your job back—he was much friendlier today."

"Yes, he treated me with the deference of a celebrity as soon as he realized I have a rare disease. You know, my story will probably be all over town by this afternoon."

"Well, that's a good thing, as long as he gets his facts straight. Chances are someone who knows you will hear and call you or come by and you'll learn more about yourself."

Judd didn't respond, but he looked uncomfortable with the idea. "What are you worried about?" she asked.

"That part of Howie's audience will be a bill collector or two."

The twist of his lips was more sardonic than serious. She wished he would be less flip and more sympathetic toward himself and his problem. "You may not like being the talk of Silver Creek, but it can only help for the time being. In fact, I'd like to take your picture, if you'll let me, and run it in the local and county papers—''

''Forget it.''

''But why?''

''I just don't like the idea. Besides, it's obvious I'm from out of town. I don't have any family around here.''

Karen wanted to argue, but the stubborn clench of his jaw warned her not to. She concentrated on the road for a while. It was a gorgeous day, cooler than yesterday, thank goodness. What would Judd have been doing this morning if the robbery last Friday hadn't interrupted his life? Fishing, maybe, since he only worked afternoons.

There was one other obvious way she could help him, and they were nearing the highway patrol office, so she couldn't wait any longer to bring it up. ''I have one more idea, and I hope you'll consider it with an open mind.''

His arm was propped in the opened window, his expression inscrutable behind his shades.

''I have an uncle in town, Ed Thomas is his name, who worked as a private eye for years, and in the Los Angeles area, too. He still takes some jobs on the side, and I'm sure he'd do a little checking for you.'' Before he could object, she added, ''He's very discreet.''

''No, thanks.''

''Oh, Judd, he's a good guy! He's my uncle.''

''It's nothing personal, Karen. I just don't like private detectives.''

''Why not? Do you know any?''

''I might,'' he said archly, ''and I don't believe in

them. Besides, he can't tell me more than the police, and I've already talked to them at length.''

Karen gave it one last shot as she pulled into the parking lot. ''My uncle lived in L.A. for twenty years. He's got a lot of friends down there, a network. Remember, Howie said you once lived in that area. Sometimes you can learn more from contacts like my uncle's than from police computers.''

Judd hesitated.

''Please say yes. Just talk to him.''

''All right. I'll talk to him.'' He waggled a finger in Karen's face. ''But the final decision whether to hire him is up to me, okay?''

''Fine, great.'' She thought of telling him Uncle Ed would work for free, because Judd was her client, but decided it was better to save that as a clincher for after Judd and Ed met.

''Are you sure you don't sell something on the side?'' he asked. ''Used cars maybe?'' He massaged his shoulder as he rotated it. ''My arm's never been twisted so skillfully.''

Judd shook his head and made a mock scowl of pain as his social worker swallowed a giggle. Potentially dangerous, he thought, how this young woman's happy glow seemed worth the discomfort her plan aroused in him. She was obviously ecstatic that he had agreed to her help, though her quivering facial muscles struggled to conceal it. She seemed so young, so disarmingly feminine in her excitement. He realized with a start that her innocence was drawing him to her, even as he felt she would be better off if she'd never met him.

Karen waited outside while Judd went in. As he stood in line to claim his car, he couldn't decide if he should allow Karen to lead him to her uncle's, or if he should tell her he'd changed his mind and send her back to her office in Granite City. True, she was being paid to play his guardian angel, but he doubted she got this wrapped up in all her clients. There were subtle signs that she felt something more for him than responsibility, possibly even more than straightforward friendship. And she wasn't the only one becoming emotionally embroiled!

Damn. It was taking forever to make his way to the head of the line. For a moment, he allowed his constant vigilance to relax and closed his eyes in weariness. But the action immediately brought a picture of Karen's face to his mind and made his pulse quicken. Karen's skin, this morning when he'd touched her cheek, had been so warm and tender. He loved the way she'd responded to him, her eyes widening first in shock, then quickly darkening to reveal a hunger even fear couldn't suppress. He'd understood her reaction to their brief physical contact, because it had closely mirrored his own. He wondered what it would be like to run his fingers through her rich, fox red hair, to slide his hands down her softly curving arms and around her waist, to feel the fullness of that beautiful bosom against his chest.

He cut off the fantasy, flicked open his eyes. The man in front of him had stepped to the desk and was arguing with the uniformed clerk about an accident report. Judd glanced about, listened to the conversation for a moment, then inexorably his thoughts slipped back to Karen and himself.

What if he already had a wife somewhere, children even, estranged perhaps, but still attached to him by ties of common experience and love? He didn't *feel* like a father, but how could he tell for sure? Reason enough to squelch any burgeoning attraction between him and Karen. Who knew what unfinished business lay in his past, what tangled relationships that might end up hurting a sensitive, virtuous woman like Karen?

With regret he considered what might have been if there weren't so many unanswered questions about his past. It would be so nice just to give in to his attraction to Karen, to enjoy being with her, to accept that his problems gave him an added reason to spend time with her. He would indulge her schemes, which were really very good ideas, like the one about the photos. Laughing with her and getting to know her would be a welcome relief from the stressful process of piecing together his memories.

Judd ground the heel of his boot into the floor, leaving a dark smear on the linoleum. To hell with all that! Karen and he must not spend time together, must not get attached. The edginess that never left his gut told him that very clearly. Because he was sure that his past held something for him and charming, innocent Karen to be truly, terrifyingly afraid of.

WHILE JUDD RETRIEVED his car, Karen called her uncle Ed from a pay phone to make sure he was in. She found him at home, rather than in his little downtown office, and took a few minutes to fill him in on Judd's case. He was immediately intrigued, and told her to come ahead with her client.

Karen led the way down the little country road on the outskirts of town, Judd following in his big Chevrolet sedan. She understood now why the men who had robbed Judd hadn't bothered to steal the car: the slate blue Impala was old enough to be a gas guzzler but not stylish enough to be a head-turning classic. It wasn't the kind of vehicle she'd expect a vintage car enthusiast to own, much less a man who brushed his teeth with boar bristles.

Karen parked in her uncle's driveway next to Ed's bottle green minivan. Judd parked up the road and walked back. The single-story brick and log homes here were widely spaced on large lots. Weathered fences lined many of the properties. A gunshot echoed in the mountain stillness, and a horse whinnied somewhere nearby.

Judd started at the sound, and Karen touched his elbow. "It's just my uncle doing some target practice. He told me he'd be out back."

She led the way around the small brick home to an unpaved, barren backyard where the dried-up weeds and grasses had been closely mowed. A stand of Douglas firs grew at the back of the property; a black-and-white paper target in the shape of a man's figure was tacked to a post in front of the trees.

"Uncle Ed," Karen called.

A burly man in his late sixties turned at her second call, raised his left hand in greeting and lowered the revolver he'd been aiming. He walked toward them, drawing the camouflage visor from his grizzled head. "Hello." He laid the gun carefully on a small table that held a box of ammunition. "How are you, honey?" He hugged Karen and kissed her cheek, then extended a beefy hand to Judd. "I'm Ed Thomas, glad to meet you."

"Judd Maxwell."

Judd's mouth was tight, forming creases in his beard, and it worried Karen. He'd acted strange when he came out of the patrol office, and only grunted when she asked about his car. Her uncle had his head cocked just a bit; she knew from experience he was sizing up her companion, but in a polite way that wasn't meant to be obvious or offensive.

"Karen didn't tell me much over the phone," Ed said, "but I understand you've had quite an experience, Mr. Maxwell. I've never talked to anyone with amnesia."

"I'd say you're in the majority," Judd responded dryly.

"We can have some coffee, if you'd like to go inside."

Judd's head moved just a fraction, taking in the secluded yard. A pair of blue jays squabbled in the trees. "No, thank you."

Ed turned and picked up his gun, busied himself with leisurely checking the chambers and reloading it. "I was just getting in a little target practice. In all my years on the job, I only had to brandish the gun once, at an irate fellow who was claiming he'd been completely disabled by a back injury at work. The insurance company hired me to follow him, and I'd just taken a video of him doing a hundred push-ups in his living room." Ed glanced up and gave his audience a wink. "When his dog started barking at me through the fence, he realized what I was up to and grabbed a baseball bat. He caught me just as I reached my car. I always kept a piece in the glove compartment, just in case." He chuckled. "I was darn glad I had it that day, too."

He faced Judd. "You do any shooting, Mr. Maxwell?"

"I'm—" Judd hesitated, then shook his head.

"You sure?" Ed said kindly. "You might not re-member." He held the gun out. "Why don't you take a try. Go ahead."

Judd wrinkled his nose at the revolver as though he'd rather handle a snake. Karen thought he might even step back as her uncle gently pushed the butt of the Smith & Wesson toward him. Karen herself didn't like guns; it had been unsettling to her the first time she witnessed her uncle practicing his favorite sport. She didn't blame Judd for not wanting to take the black grip.

"Most men around here are hunters, rifle users," Ed explained. "I can never find anyone for some friendly competition with a handgun."

As Judd continued to hesitate, Karen felt an impulse to wrap her arm around him and protect him. She realized Ed was just trying to break the ice, to get Judd focused on something other than his amnesia in order to relax him, but she wished he'd chosen a different method.

Ed made an urging motion, an encouraging smile on his face. Judd frowned in resignation and slowly reached out, took the butt of the revolver. Ed scurried to affix a new paper target before the trees, then ushered his guest to a mark in the grass before moving back to stand with his niece.

The late morning sun was high in the sky, and it was hot. Judd's shirt clung to the middle of his back as he spread his legs slightly, clasped both hands around the grip and pointed straight at the target. It had gone very still in the yard; the jays had flown away. The sensation of someone walking over her grave shivered Karen's spine as she watched the dark-haired, powerfully muscled man take careful aim. She wanted to turn her head but couldn't. She braced for the explosion.

Judd's first shot missed the target completely, lodging in one of the tightly packed firs beyond it. Karen exhaled, grateful to learn he had no affinity with firearms.

Ed cleared his throat. "Ah, good try, son. To the right and a little high. Try again."

Judd obediently took two more shots; the third one just nicked the edge of the target.

Judd dropped his arms, walked to the table and laid the gun down. He pulled a bandanna handkerchief from his back pocket and wiped the sweat from his brow. "Thank you for the hospitality, Mr. Thomas. I've had a dull headache all morning, and the sun seems to have made it worse. Why don't you give me your card, and I'll call you if I need your services."

Ed pulled out his wallet, and with a nod, handed Judd his business card.

Karen looked into Judd's face in concern. "Are you okay? You should call Dr. Bergman if you're not feeling well. I've got his number."

"No, I just need to lie down for a bit, Karen. Thanks for the ride this morning."

Karen was loath to let him go, but whether he genuinely had a headache, or was using it as an excuse to avoid discussing his problem with her uncle, she could tell it would be useless to argue with him.

"Call me if you need anything," she said, and added, "I'll be in touch."

Ed watched Judd as the younger man retreated around the side of the house. "An interesting performance." He put his arm around his niece's shoulders. "Come on, pumpkin, let's get some coffee. I think you'd better tell me everything you know about this fellow."

They entered the house and passed through the living room with its single recliner and wide-screen TV. Ed had never married, and he'd rarely visited his hometown after his younger brother, Karen's father, died when Karen was a baby. Three years ago, when her mother had passed away, Ed had accepted Karen's invitation to stay at her house for the funeral and, to Karen's surprise, had extended his visit for several weeks. It had naturally been a wrenching time for Karen, but she and her uncle had gotten along well from the start. When he abruptly announced he'd decided to retire and move to Silver Creek, Karen had been delighted. He seemed to be enjoying the relaxed summers and coping with the snowy winters and had never once complained to her about his decision.

"I'm trying to figure out our friend Maxwell," Ed said as he poured them coffee at the breakfast table.

"Everyone is, including himself, I'm sure."

Ed harrumphed. "He may know more about himself than he lets on. I'm almost sure he's experienced with a gun."

Karen laughed. "But surely, it was obvious he couldn't hit the side of a barn."

"Did you see the way he held the gun, straight in front, both hands? I've done instructing at rifle ranges over the years, as a sideline. Ninety-five percent of novices want to hold the gun in their right hand, straight out, like they do in Western movies."

Something stirred in Karen's stomach. "So, maybe he doesn't watch Westerns."

Ed was gazing into the distance. "He was very smooth. He could have put the bullet in the ground, but he was off just enough each time to make it look like he was trying. He may have been attempting to deceive me."

"Why would he do that? He could have learned to shoot in the service or the reserves or any number of other places, and he's just rusty. The fact he doesn't like guns was plain when you offered it to him. And it just occurred to me—" she slapped the table "—the man or men who robbed him may have used guns. It could be a big part of the reason he blacked out in the first place, if they really threatened to shoot him. I hope we haven't unwittingly traumatized him again!"

She told Ed everything she'd learned about Judd up to last night. When she finished, Ed asked, "Do you have any information that would suggest why he was parked there on the shoulder of the highway, or what caused the amnesia?"

She was reluctant to mention Judd's fight with his boss. She'd just witnessed how suspicious Ed could be, probably a result of having spent most of his life chasing insurance defrauders and unfaithful husbands. However, there wasn't any way to avoid it. She told him what Howie had revealed about Judd's movements Friday night. "The point is," she concluded, "someone could have overheard their conversation at the station and watched Judd take off with a wallet full of cash. The robber could have followed him and run him off the road, then forced him to hand over the money at gunpoint."

Ed rose to get himself another coffee. "It's a neat theory. I suppose having someone threaten to blow your head off would be terrifying, but it happens somewhere every day, and the victims don't usually react by forgetting their entire past lives. More?'' He held the pot up to Karen, who checked her watch and shook her head. He continued, ''Your scenario fits the facts, but we have to ask why he was in such a hurry to get the cash. Apparently it was important enough that he was willing to give his job up for it. It sounds like he was in some kind of big trouble—blackmail, or drugs maybe.''

''Oh, Uncle Ed. Surely it's obvious that Judd is the victim here, not the bad guy. You don't have to be suspicious of him. Even if Judd was hiding the fact he can use a gun, there could be half a dozen good reasons for it.''

Ed narrowed his eyes at her. ''That's the first time I've ever heard you say there's a good reason for lying. Maybe you'd better ask someone else in your office to handle this case.''

Darn, Karen thought. He was sensing her attraction to Judd. She didn't want him worrying about her, or adding to the ridiculous seed of doubt he'd planted in her. ''There's no need for me to transfer the case,'' she said in a detached, professional tone. She checked her watch again. ''I'm sorry, Uncle Ed, I've got an appointment in Granite at one, and I'm already late.''

As Ed showed her to the door, he said, ''Even though he hasn't hired me, I can see what I can dig up on Judd's past, try to locate his ex-wife or something, if you still want me to.''

She recognized his treatment of her as an adult to be an olive branch. She gave him a brief hug. ''Yes, I'd appreciate that. Judd needs your help, and I'm sure he was just too flustered by the target practice to ask for it. I'll wait for an opportune moment and tell him I gave you the go-ahead.''

He paused with one hand on the doorknob. ''I know you feel sorry for this fella, honey, and you've got a heart of gold for folks in trouble, but do something, *for me*. Be cautious. I've been in the PI business for almost thirty years, and instinct tells me there's something not right about Judd Maxwell.''

Chapter Five

Karen's entire day got turned around when she returned home for a quick lunch. There was a message on her answering machine from the receptionist at her office, saying that her one-o'clock appointment had been canceled. Karen called the office and found she had no other messages.

Before hanging up the phone, she decided to put in a call to Dr. Bergman at St. Mary's. To her good fortune, the doctor was in and had ten minutes to spare. To satisfy her uncle's fears, she asked Bergman if Judd could be faking the amnesia out of some ulterior motive. The psychiatrist answered that, in his best medical opinion, Judd was not malingering.

The canceled appointment having left her afternoon free, she ate a leisurely lunch and decided she'd better deposit her paycheck and run some errands while she had the chance. She was leaving her bank on Main Street when she spotted Judd Maxwell's car, parked half a block away.

Her pulse quickened at the thought he was nearby. What were her chances of ''running into him'' if she tried to find him? She crossed the street and began looking in the storefronts.

He was standing at a teller's window in the savings and loan. Karen smoothed the hair around her face in the reflection of the glass before entering the double doors.

Judd was waiting for the absent teller to return, but rather than lounging against the counter in a relaxed manner, his legs were spread and back straight, like a Marine at ease.

He turned at her approach, and a smile split his face. He'd removed his sunglasses, and the warm greeting in his eyes, so unfamiliar and unexpected, made her heart take flight.

"What are you doing here?" he asked.

"I was about to ask you the same thing. I saw your car outside. My afternoon appointment came down with the flu, so I didn't have to go in to Granite after all. Do you have an account here?"

"Yes, thank goodness. Why does such a little town need seven banking establishments? I've been making the rounds, asking at each one if I'd ever done business there."

"How many have you already been to?"

"Six."

Karen laughed, sharing in the happy relief his wry expression conveyed. It struck her afresh how anxious she was to see Judd get back on his feet. Dr. Bergman had encouraged her to continue firmly but patiently offering Judd her friendship and understanding. She hadn't mentioned it to the doctor, but she had a definite feeling there was a stable, very personable character behind Judd's changeable, often wary exterior. Thank goodness she hadn't allowed herself to get discouraged by his moods! If she'd hesitated to look for him when she spotted his car, they wouldn't be sharing this moment of discovery.

"Thank you for waiting," a middle-aged woman said as she joined them on the other side of the counter. "I have your signature card here, sir." The teller compared Judd's penmanship with her sample, then typed some information onto her computer screen. "You have a regular checking account with us, no other accounts. The checking balance is two dollars, three cents."

"That's all?"

"Yes, not including any deposits made today."

"I haven't made any."

The teller glanced up, noted Judd's stunned expression, then hit the scroll key. "The most recent activity on the account was…last Friday. Three hundred eighty dollars was withdrawn from the ATM."

"What time Friday?"

"Um, 6:32 p.m."

"Thank you."

Judd's whole countenance had fallen, and it made Karen feel sick. She touched his arm as they walked through the lobby. "I know that's not news you wanted to hear, but you won't be broke forever. I'm sure, with your skills, we can find you another job—"

He stopped and turned to face her with hard eyes. "That's not the problem."

"It's not?"

Judd glanced about sharply, but there was no one near to overhear. He dropped his voice. "Haven't you wondered why I demanded my pay from Summers Friday night? Why I drained my bank account at the same time? Why they didn't find even a suitcase in the trunk of my car? I was in one big hurry to get out of town, Karen. I was, probably still am, in some kind of deep trouble.''

It took her a moment to formulate an answer. Though she'd found Judd's physical presence somewhat menacing in the first minutes she met him, it had never occurred to her he might have a police record. He just hadn't struck her as that type of man.

''But surely,'' she began, ''if the police wanted to arrest you, they would have done it as soon as they identified you at the hospital.'' His fevered look warned her he was ready to bolt, and she talked faster. ''Listen, there are a lot of perfectly good explanations why you could have needed that money on the spur of the moment. Maybe you got a call that your mother was very sick and you needed a ticket on the first flight out. When my mom came down with cancer a couple of years ago, I would have begged, borrowed or stolen to get to her side.'' She immediately regretted the choice of words, but hoped he would overlook it and consider her point.

''Karen.'' He took her earnestly by the forearms, his big hands clasping her skin beneath the short sleeves of her blouse. She didn't look down, but every nerve ending in her body seemed wired to her arms. His palms were damp with anxiety, but his grip was sure and the pressure of his fingers overwhelmingly masculine.

''You've been wonderful to me, and I appreciate your desire to help me. But you don't understand everything that's going on here.'' His gray eyes riveted her with earnestness. ''Despite what you feel for me, whether it's compassion, or duty, or something more personal—''

Karen blushed, understanding perfectly his meaning.

"Believe me, it's not worth you staying involved with me." He paused a moment, grinding his jaw. "There's nothing that says I have to accept social services' help, is there?"

"No," she admitted.

"Then in that case, I'm hereby refusing any further assistance. And I don't want you coming around on your time off, either," he added, perhaps reading her mind.

What could she say? The steel in his eyes told her she'd better not argue, and causing a scene here in the bank would only embarrass him.

However, the thought of letting him go was almost unbearable. Until he'd come out and put it into words a few moments ago, she hadn't realized how personally attracted she was to him.

For the first time, his gaze faltered. He looked down, then back up, but couldn't quite meet her eyes. "Goodbye." And with that he left.

Karen's throat ached as she watched him go. To manage her crushing disappointment, she told herself fiercely this wasn't the end. She wasn't about to stop checking on him just because he was confused and imagined himself a burden to others. She shouldn't take his rejection personally. After all, hadn't Dr. Bergman warned her that feelings of unease, even paranoia, were normal for a victim of amnesia?

As she walked to her car, Karen had to admit that some of the things Judd had learned were disturbing. Besides the mysterious business with the money, she herself had wondered why, with all his intelligence and obvious drive, he had worked only part-time as an auto mechanic. She'd wondered if he had a second job Howie didn't know about, or did some kind of volunteer work in his spare time, or was a closet composer or something. But seen from Judd's depressed perspective, his scant employment history might suggest he was an aimless drifter, even a troublemaker, without a taste for work or responsibility. It *was* a possibility, but Karen just couldn't buy it.

As she stepped into her car, she suddenly felt a terrific impatience for Judd's memory to return. Once she knew who he was, she'd have a better idea where she stood with him. Part of her had tingled at every suggestion that he wasn't attached, the same part of her that had avoided imagining him with another woman.

Karen sighed and told herself she was asking for a letdown by falling for a man with an unknown past.

"You should be doing better, resisting that magnetic pull of his," she said aloud at the stoplight, "given all the experience you've had!" In twenty-six years, how many Mr. Wrongs had she side-stepped? She briefly went down the list of men she'd dated who were emotionally mature, responsible and well employed, but almost totally disinterested in doing anything but tending to their own success and comfort. Helping others had always been important to her, something she felt she owed to fellow members of the human family. Though she was getting older and the pool of marriageable men was shrinking, she still wasn't ready to compromise and marry someone who didn't share her values.

JUDD LAY AWAKE for a long time that night. By his bed, the face of the cheap digital alarm clock glowed

1:05. The walls of the former motel were thin; he'd lain awake for the past hour, listening to the neighbor's television after switching off his own. Now, apparently, the other party had gone to bed, too. In this quiet residential section of town, there wasn't even the sound of a car passing on the street. Judd almost wished his neighbor had decided to pull an all-nighter.

Judd got up in his boxers and padded quietly across the carpet. There was no sound from the wrought-iron birdcage, covered with a dark cloth, as he passed. The lively cockatiel, whom Judd had christened "Trouble," had proved to be an affectionate pet. He constantly begged to be let out of his cage to ride companionably around the apartment on Judd's shoulder. But with the setting sun, Trouble had rested his head on his back and tucked up one leg like a flamingo, ready for slumber. Judd had whispered "Good night" as he carefully arranged the cage cover and received a sleepy peep in response.

Had Trouble stirred now, Judd probably would have taken him out for company. But the bird had been kept awake much of last night by his owner's noisome nightmares, and Judd felt the poor cockatiel deserved a rest.

Judd drew himself a glass of water in the kitchenette, then stood at the crack in the front curtains, staring out at the scraggly lawn and deeply shadowed street. He felt so alone. Alone with a thousand questions that wouldn't let him sleep. Alone without even himself for company. *Who was he?*

After the disastrous episode at the private investigator's house, he'd come home and tried to eat something, tried to relax while he regrouped. But the apartment itself disturbed him. By all accounts, he made barely enough money to live on, yet his personal possessions were expensive. The British-made CD player, amplifier and mahogany speakers showed no signs of wear and convinced him he'd acquired the pieces quite recently. Had he purchased them from some high-end stereo store in Granite, or had they ''fallen off a truck''? Was he a thief or a masked robber of convenience stores? An escaped criminal with the law on his heels? If so, why were the authorities allowing him to roam free?

His lunch of canned beans half-eaten, he had grabbed his car keys and gone downtown to look for his bank, armed with his temporary, replacement driver's license, hoping the tellers would accept it as identification.

The helpful clerk at the highway-patrol office had issued the license to him that morning. It seemed everyone in the small outpost, which also served as a Department of Motor Vehicles, was familiar with his case. The clerk had helped him with the paperwork and looked up his driving record. That's when she'd given him the news he had a driver's license in three other western states.

The status of his checking account had been even more ominous. Knowing he had needed money Friday night, he had been prepared today for the worst as he made the round of the banks and savings and loans. But when Karen walked up with that room-lighting smile, he'd suddenly been swept away by the illogical, but powerful, notion that nothing could go wrong while she was with him. If only!

What threat had caused him to gather every dime he had and take off Friday night? Who or what had he been fleeing from on Highway 18? If he could just find out his movements between seven-fifteen, when he left Howie's garage, and midnight, when the officers found him, he might be able to recall everything.

Judd ran a hand through his hair. Virtually nothing had jogged his memory so far. It was like the damn brain cells that held the information had just died. Today, when Ed Thomas handed him that gun… God help him, he'd felt genuine terror. Staring at the man-shaped target, he *knew* he could hit it directly through the heart, or the abdomen, or anywhere else he chose. He'd been filled with irrational fears as he raised the gun, afraid if he pierced the silhouette that blood would spew forth!

Judd leaned his sweating forehead against the cold glass, his breath heavy and ragged in his ears. Heaven help him, was he going insane?

He finally staggered back to his bed and fell down on it.

And then he started suffocating. He was alone, in a dark, impenetrable, very humid place. Lights— vague, fuzzy balls—appeared in the distance and slowly grew. He tried to make out what they were. They appeared to be the flattened shapes of women, with their arms out. He didn't want to look at them anymore, but they kept advancing, like paper targets being retrieved on a wire. The women frightened him, and he closed his eyes, began shooting. When he dared look again, he realized the first bloody target had come to rest before him—it had Karen's smiling face.

IT WAS MIDMORNING, and the burly apartment man-ager knew he was about to be throttled. Judd saw the fear in the other man's eyes, the whites standing out in the East Indian's face. Judd gave a laughing snort and inched closer to his landlord, who stepped back. "You don't have the guts to throw me out, do you?"

"Mr. Maxwell, I will call the police if you continue to threaten me." He had a precise way of speaking and a slight British accent, thickened now by his anxiety.

"If you make it to the phone fast enough."

"Mr. Maxwell, please!"

The door of a nearby unit opened three inches, revealing a mother with a small child at her knee. As the woman watched them anxiously though the crack, Judd lowered his hands to his sides, forced his fists to unclench.

The landlord, having also noticed the woman, raised his voice. "I desire no trouble. If you have the rent money now and give it to me, I will allow you to stay."

Judd's irritation flared again. "I told you, I haven't got the money. Not any of it."

"But you promised me a check would come for you last Friday, so I gave you the extra time. The rent is now over two weeks past due, and the neighbors are complaining about your nightmares. They cannot sleep the last two nights, with your moaning and calling out and your pet bird screeching." The Indian looked sympathetic, in spite of himself. "It is frightening to them, Mr. Maxwell. I cannot afford to let you stay on without paying, *and* risk losing other tenants if your night terrors continue."

If he took time out to think about it, Judd knew he'd probably agree with the man, say he was within his rights, but Judd didn't feel like being rational or agreeable or civilized at the moment. He wanted to ball up his fists again and beat the life out of someone.

He stepped back, grabbed the doorknob. "I'll be out by this afternoon," he said, and slammed the door.

NO ONE ANSWERED Karen's knock as she stood in front of Judd's apartment, about an hour before noon. The curtains were closed, but Judd's car was parked outside. Karen shifted the bag of groceries to her hip and tried the knob—it wasn't locked. She rapped again, called out, "Judd, it's Karen," and let herself in.

A cheery greeting died on her lips as she surveyed the room. Clothes were strewed everywhere on the floor and over the twisted sheets of the bed, like a tornado had caught them up and hurled them. Judd ignored her as he grabbed a shirt from the floor.

"What happened here?"

Judd wadded the garment in his hands and glared at her. "I'm not in the mood for visitors this morning, Karen."

"I can see that." She ducked into the kitchen, slipped the eggs and milk into the refrigerator and left the rest of the groceries on the counter. When she came out, Judd was shoving clothes into a canvas duffel on the bed.

"Are you going somewhere?"

"Yes, to Bedlam."

"I'd say you're already there." Her attempt at humor fell flat. Karen bit her nail and tried to think how to not antagonize him further. "Can you tell me when you'll be back?"

"No. I'm not going on a cruise, and I'm not coming back. I've been evicted."

"Evicted! Oh, Judd, no. How did that happen?"

"The easiest and fastest way—I didn't pay my rent, apparently."

Karen didn't use oaths, but she felt like uttering one now. "Where will you go?"

"I have no idea." He picked up the alarm clock, examined it as if trying to decide whether it was his or belonged to the apartment, then slammed it down on the nightstand. "I'm sure if I wander around long enough I'll find a bridge somewhere I can sleep under."

He was being facetious, and Karen knew it. "Don't be silly." She picked a sock from the floor, began looking for its mate.

Judd glanced over his shoulder. "Leave that. I can do it myself. You'd better go."

"No. I'm going to find you a place to stay."

Judd threw down a pair of shoes and rounded on her. "I can take care of myself!"

Karen, too, felt her control slip. "How?" she yelled back. "By becoming a street person?"

"I'd rather live on the streets somewhere else than stay in Silver Creek to be treated like a freak."

"Oh, for goodness' sake, Judd, be reasonable! At every turn, you've fought me—'No, I can't do that, no, I can't let you do this,'" she mimicked. She thought she saw Judd's mouth twitch a hair. His blood was still up, but some of the fire left his eye.

"For a little thing," he said, taking a step toward her, "you're awful sure of yourself, aren't you?"

The argument had cleared her head, and she suddenly felt very light. She closed the room-length gap between them a pace. "I don't claim to have all the answers, but you could at least try working with me instead of against me, for a change."

"That's your advice, then?" His tone was normal again, almost teasing.

"Yes." They were slowly inching closer. "And that you give up your foolish pride for a few days."

"You think I've been foolish?"

He was only half an arm's length from her now. Looking up into his amused, faintly smoldering eyes, she thought he didn't seem immature at all. "Not foolish, normal rather. Dr. Bergman says so."

She tried to hang on to her thoughts, but his gaze fascinated her; his irises were dark pewter, flecked with silver. Without touching her, he seemed to be reaching out to capture her, wrapping invisible arms around her middle. She knew in her bones he would kiss her if she came any closer.

She licked her lips. "It's, ah, normal for amnesia victims to be angry, even paranoid."

For a moment, he seemed not to be listening, but then his expression changed. Surprise flickered across his face. She leaned toward him, inviting his embrace.

"Dr. Bergman said that?" he asked quietly, voice altered.

"Yes, you're a textbook case. That's what he said."

Judd put his hands lightly on her shoulders. "He never said anything like that to me—he was mostly frustrated he couldn't get me to go under. You've been a lot more patient," he finished huskily.

Karen wondered dreamily if there was a double meaning to the words. She hadn't admitted it to herself before now, but she *had* been waiting for his kiss. "Yes," she breathed, parting her lips just slightly, closing her eyes.

His mouth brushed hers, tender and warm, lingering only as long as might be appropriate to express gratitude and thanks. The kiss thrilled her, and left her wanting more. She leaned toward him again, into empty space, and opened her eyes. Judd had moved back, his expression turned inward and thoughtful, apparently digesting what she'd just said about his amnesia.

Karen stepped away, covering the awkwardness she felt as his hands released her shoulders. "I'm, ah, sorry Dr. Bergman didn't discuss your case with you more." She shoved her hands in the pockets of her skirt. "I have to say that I agree with what he told me." She slipped into social worker's jargon, giving him a speech she'd often recited. "In my experience with people under extreme stress, who have been dispossessed from their homes and familiar surroundings, fear and anger are very common."

Judd sat down on a dinette chair, leaned his elbows on his knees. "I've been having terrible nightmares —another reason they want me out of here. I even terrified poor Trouble. I woke up twice last night in a cold sweat and found him on the bottom of his cage, flapping around. I was afraid he'd hurt himself."

"More reason not to take off," Karen said gently, laying a hand on his shoulder for a moment. "Who would care for Trouble?"

"You've got a point. But where can I go? I doubt Howie Summers would rent me a room."

His tone was joking, rather than sarcastic as he'd been earlier, and Karen chuckled. She shrugged the tension from her shoulders as she sat down at the table with him, and they talked about his experience at the hospital, and his frustration that nothing so far had helped his memory return. She didn't want to discourage him, but now was the time to tell him what Dr. Bergman had warned her about, that it could take a couple of weeks for the amnesia to break, even longer for it to clear up completely. She was pleased when Judd received the news with equanimity.

"You're not disappointed?" she asked.

"No, maybe even the reverse. I'm beginning to wonder if I haven't been expecting too much of myself. It's unreasonable to think I could come down with amnesia, and wake up the next morning feeling right as rain."

"That's right," she said quietly. An intimacy had grown up between them as they talked about his illness. Karen could feel the bond growing between them.

Judd reached out and took her hand. "I know I've given you a rough time, Karen, and I'm sorry."

Karen blushed with pleasure. "Well, it's been understandable. Just try to lighten up. Everything will work out."

Unlike his earlier touches, which had shot through her like charges of sexual electricity, his grasp now filled her with a sense of quiet happiness and well-being. Strange that she should feel this way with someone she'd just met. It didn't seem possible that she knew so little about his past—at this moment, she felt as though she had loved and lived with him for a long time.

But Judd broke the spell. "We should talk about what happened a few minutes ago," he said. "I kissed you, and to be perfectly honest, I'm not sure I had any right to."

"Why is that?" She was suddenly afraid he knew something she didn't.

"Besides the fact that we still haven't learned much about my past, it's not certain that I don't have a…family…out there somewhere. I haven't found any photos around, and you heard Howie Summers say he thought I was divorced. Well, those seem like good signs. But until I'm sure…you see, I'm beginning to care about you very much…and the last thing I'd want you to think is that I'm taking advantage of you."

He started to withdraw his hand from hers, but Karen didn't let go. "I care about you, too," she said. She was impressed at how brutally honest he was willing to be, and how honorable. But feeling the way she did about him at this moment, she couldn't bring herself to match his candor.

"I'm not worried," she fibbed. "The chances you're attached are very slim." With greater conviction, she added, "I know whatever we discover about your past, it can only be good." She leaned forward and kissed him on the cheek, smelling the attractive tang of his aftershave mixed with the earthy scent of his skin.

As she got up from the table, she cleared her throat and glanced at her watch. "I should start making some calls if I'm going to find you a place to stay. Can I use your phone?"

"Of course, thank you. I'll finish packing."

Karen pulled a pen and notepad from her purse, then dialed her office. She always carried the phone numbers of the nursing homes in Granite County that took patients on full government assistance, but she had to ask the secretary at work where she could place an able-bodied man in his thirties. The list was short: a couple of halfway houses for recovering alcoholics and drug addicts, and Granite City's single homeless shelter. As she'd feared, the two house managers told her they were fully booked, with a waiting list of at least a month. Karen had been called out twice to interview elderly street people who wandered into the downtown shelter and knew the facility could probably offer Judd a bed, but only for a few nights, and they had no facilities for storing his belongings, much less a cockatiel in an iron cage.

Karen decided against calling the homeless shelter and chewed on her thumbnail as she thought. She didn't believe Judd would want to stay at her uncle Ed's house, and given Ed's suspicious attitude toward Judd, it wasn't a good idea, anyway. She had a former boyfriend who was a mining engineer and had a nice two-bedroom apartment in town, but Mark wasn't the helping-hand kind, and he'd probably be flabbergasted if she called him.

Even though it was a little unorthodox, and her boss would give her a lecture if he found out, there was really only one place Karen could think of for Judd to go for the next week or two.

"Judd."

He was clearing out the medicine cabinet. "So, have you booked me into the Pariah Palace?"

"No, and I'm afraid the Halfway Hilton was full up, too. Unless we, ah, opt for the bridge idea, you'll have to stay at my place."

Chapter Six

"*Your* place? You're joking."

"No." She told him about the recovery houses but didn't mention the homeless shelter.

"I can't inconvenience you."

Karen braced herself for another confrontation with his familiar stubborn streak. "It will only be for a few days, and you won't be any trouble at all. You can sleep on the sofa and help with the chores."

"It's too much."

"No, it's not. I was going to have to take your pet bird, anyway." She'd have to deal with her cat, Toby, when the time came. "They don't allow animals at men's houses, you know. So why shouldn't I take the owner, too?"

Judd shifted to one hip. "I, ah, geez. This is getting more complicated all the time."

"Please, Judd. Do this for me. I don't want to worry about you, and you know I will if you go off somewhere on your own."

Judd weakened. "All right," he said slowly, "but I don't want to park myself on you a moment longer than is necessary. And when I get a job, I'll pay you back for the room and board."

When she started to protest, he pointed a finger at her, sighting down it with a fierce no-arguments look.

A FEAST AWAITED Karen when she arrived home from the office that night. After showing Judd where she lived, giving him an extra key and telling him to make himself at home, she'd had to dash to Granite City.

While she was at work, Judd had packed his stuff in cardboard boxes and stacked them in Karen's garage. The house only had one bedroom, the second one having been eliminated at some point to open up the living room and allow space for a dining table. Judd's suitcase sat on a chair next to the sleeper sofa.

Looking about as she stepped in the door, Karen was suddenly reminded of one of her friends from college and the girl's romantic description of how she felt the day her fiancé moved in. Karen had never made love with a man, much less considered living with one. But she hadn't thought twice about inviting Judd here.

Judd was in the kitchen searing the steaks he'd brought from his apartment. Karen could smell potatoes baking, and a pot simmered on the stove. Karen popped in to say hello, then showered and changed into shorts and a fresh blouse while he finished cooking. When she reentered the living room, Judd was staring out the windows to the sunporch, the washed skillet and a dish towel in his hands.

He started as he turned, his eyes widening slightly.

"I'm sorry. I didn't mean to sneak up on you."

"You didn't. I heard you coming. I'm just impressed with how..." From his foxy grin, she thought he was going to say *sexy,* but he finished, "how beautiful you look."

His eyes lingered on her a moment, then he glanced back at the sunporch.

"What were you looking at?" she asked.

He sucked in his breath, his wide chest visibly expanding beneath the white polo shirt. "Nothing. I just thought I heard a car pull up, in your back alley, and idle there for a few minutes. It's gone now. Probably just someone picking up one of your neighbors."

Karen knew that none of her neighbors used the unpaved alley to exit their homes, but she didn't say so. Judd didn't seem too concerned about his observation, and she certainly didn't want to fuel his amnesia-induced paranoia again.

They listened to music as they ate. Judd had obviously played with her tiny living room stereo, because it was tuned to a pleasant light rock station Karen was unfamiliar with, the FM signal coming in remarkably strong. Judd seemed more interested in eating than talking, while Karen felt keyed up and strangely at a loss for topics of conversation.

Though she'd eaten dinner at this same table for years, with Judd catercorner from her, the experience felt strange and new, and more than a little exciting. It amazed her that, barely hours after accepting her invitation, Judd had filled her bachelorette home with his masculine presence. She was listening to his music, eating the food he'd prepared with his gourmet cookware, watching his pet bird in its cage across from them in the living room.

It was almost as though he'd come to stay. A premonition struck her that he had moved into her life and would change not only her surroundings but her, too, making her a part of *his* world.

It gave her the titillating sensation of being a new woman. At the same time, she told herself it was foolish to jump ahead. Foolish, and potentially hurt-ful, if it turned out Judd wasn't free. There was still a possibility he might wake up from his amnesia and remember he was deeply in love with someone else.

"Would you like a steak knife?" she asked, push-ing the disheartening thought away.

"No, thank you." She got herself one, then watched as Judd cut through his steak, cleaving the meat like butter. He took big bites of the rare steak, chewing with relish, then washed it down with a swallow of beer, tilting his head back as he grasped the bottle by the neck. He held the liquid in his mouth for a moment to taste it before swallowing it.

When he noticed her watching him, he gave her an amused, knowing grin. She blushed and looked away, then tried to concentrate on Trouble, who was eating his own dinner of bird pellets. When she looked Judd's way again, on the excuse he might need another helping of vegetables, she caught him paused with fork in hand, studying *her* profile. Now it was his turn to look away. Karen felt as though the temperature in the room had risen at least ten degrees.

As they finished their meal, the charged silence became too much for her. Karen asked Judd how he'd managed to get Trouble's cage in his car. He leaned forward on his elbows, the pine tabletop creaking under the weight of his muscled torso. He proceeded to delight her with the story of how he'd easily broken the iron cage down with a screwdriver, then been flummoxed as to how to transport the bird. After a too personal, and volubly resented, inspection of Trouble's wings, Judd had determined they were clipped and the cockatiel was probably incapable of flying away. Therefore, Judd had taken the line of least resistance and simply carried Trouble on his shoulder in the car.

"You're kidding?"

Judd swallowed his last bite of steak. She noticed the deliberate, masculine movements of his hands as he brushed his lips with the paper napkin and pushed back his plate. "No, I think Trouble enjoyed the trip. He was almost asleep when we got here, he was so relaxed. It was like he does it all the time."

"I doubt that. At least not in town. You'd be famous if the two of you were in the habit of driving around like Bluebeard and Polly."

Judd chuckled, the baritone rumble coming from deep in his chest. Karen smiled to herself and tipped her head; with his dark hair and beard now grown in very nicely, he rather looked the part of a pirate. Yes, very rakish indeed.

She realized she was feeling a little sassy after the satisfying meal, and Judd's presence was giving her more pleasure and a greater sense of being alive than she could ever remember. The reminder that they were very much alone kept running through her mind, teasing her with provocative possibilities that made her pulse race and start. Trying to act natural and not flirt with him was getting harder by the minute.

She cleared her throat. "By the way, did you get any calls before you left?"

"No. I'll call the phone company tomorrow about turning off the service."

"Perhaps we could have your calls diverted here."

Judd shook his head. "Thanks, but I think it would be a waste of time. I don't want to sound pessimistic, but if anyone really wants to find me, I left your address with the landlord."

She suddenly wondered if Judd had really been as much of a loner as circumstances seemed to indicate. He was personable and had a good sense of humor when he allowed himself to show it. It seemed strange he hadn't made at least one or two friends in the months he'd spent here; Silver Creek was a friendly little town… She realized again that the two of them were all alone here. What had been a stirring thought made her vaguely uneasy for a moment.

Judd rose and started to clear away the plates.

"No, let me do that," she said, eager for something to do to shake off her unwelcome doubts. "Why don't you sit on the back porch—it's screened to keep the mosquitoes out—and I'll join you in a minute."

He offered to help her with the dishes, but she insisted.

It took her only a few minutes to clean up the kitchen, and by then her moment of unease was forgotten. When she went out to the porch, he was leaning against the framing, looking up into the night sky, and for a moment, Karen studied him. His profile, backlit by the moon, was strong, and powerful arms were crossed over his chest. He was so solid, so capable and clearly used to being his own master. It seemed impossible that a man such as this could be afflicted with any mental infirmity, much less total loss of memory! She wouldn't have believed it if someone had pointed him out on the street and told her.

"Would you like some coffee, or tea maybe?" she asked quietly.

He turned, white teeth flashing. "No, thanks. I'm looking forward to an undisturbed night's sleep tonight."

"If you'd like to retire now—"

"No, it's too nice out here, and I'd much rather talk for a while."

Karen's stomach flip-flopped with pleasure, and she told him, "Me, too."

There were a couple of rickety lawn chairs, and a big, old-fashioned swing was chained to the porch rafters. Her professional conscience urged her to take one of the chairs, but another, more beguiling voice, tempted her to live dangerously. She lowered herself onto the end of the swing and crossed her ankles underneath. Her legs felt deliciously cool in shorts after wearing panty hose all day.

Judd joined her. Her respiration quickened as he settled into the opposite corner of the swing, resting his right thigh on the seat between them so he could face her. He gently rocked the swing with his outstretched leg, then leaned back, his left hand holding the chain, and closed his eyes.

After the heat of the day, the evening was pleasantly balmy. The flowered scent of Karen's baby powder mixed with the ever present mountain pine to perfume the air. The resident blue jays had settled in for the night, and the only sound was the gentle throbbing of the stereo from the living room.

"It feels good to relax," Judd said. "I haven't felt

this at ease since…'' He searched his mind, then chuckled and added, ''Since I can't remember when.''

She wanted to tell him that his words closely mirrored her own thoughts during dinner, and that she hoped her presence had something to do with his rejuvenation, just as he was making her feel so happy, but all she said was, ''It's good to see you this way.''

Judd looked seriously at her. ''I want to thank you, Karen, for our talk this morning, and for bearing with my moods—'' he stayed her as she began shaking her head in denial that he'd been a problem ''—and for opening your home to me. I know you're going to say you don't deserve any gratitude and that you've just been doing your job, but letting me stay here is not, I am sure, in your job description. In short, thanks for having faith in me.''

''It's no big deal, really. I'm sure you would have done the same if you were me.''

''I don't know.'' He stared into the distance. ''From what I remember, the ability to trust is a rare quality these days, and not many people are willing to take the risk. I'm not sure what kind of life I led before, but I have a feeling I was pretty hardened when it came to believing in other people.''

''Perhaps you were just solitary by nature. Some folks are.''

''And some become that way, because of what life does to them. Perhaps it was like that for me.''

Karen knew she should feel glad that Judd was opening up to her, finally trusting her. But she was suddenly tired of playing his caseworker. His overt masculinity had stirred the woman in her, and the night was making her long for something quite different, even forbidden, from him. He'd kissed her once before. Would he want to again?

"Is anything wrong?" he asked abruptly.

Had he read her mind? She wanted to tell him how much she cared about him, but she also wanted the first move to be his. In confusion all she could think to say was, "What?"

"You were frowning just now, like I'd said the wrong thing."

"No, not exactly. I'm sorry." She threw up her hands in a gesture of frustration. "I'm very glad you're feeling better—it's wonderful." How could she talk around the issue? "It's just that, well...do you think it's possible to get tired of having a Florence Nightingale reputation?"

Judd grinned. "Florence Nightingale, eh? Let me try to remember. Wasn't she a perpetual spinster?"

"I'm afraid you hit it on the head. She was every dying soldier's sister."

He stretched his arm along the swing back and toyed with the shoulder of her short-sleeved blouse. "But you told me the other day you usually work with seniors, not younger men, and surely your boyfriends haven't treated you that way?"

"Haven't they?" She couldn't believe she felt comfortable enough with a man to say that.

"That's impossible!" He looked satisfyingly astonished.

"Well, not *all* my boyfriends have treated me like a pal. There was the up-and-coming mining engineer who wanted to marry me. His plan was that, following his next promotion, we'd move to the state capital, where he could get a really high-paying job, and

I would progress to a desk job and eventually become an assistant director of the state Social Services Department, so between us we could afford to live happily ever after in a five-thousand-square-foot home. Which neither of us would spend any time in, much less playing with our children, because we'd both be too busy working!''

"Sounds like the guy needed an accountant, not a woman."

She liked the way he said "a woman" rather than "a wife."

"When I told him what social workers make in salary," she continued, "Mark almost choked. I think he instantly regretted he'd proposed. He told me he thought all government workers were on the gravy train. I had to tell him that social workers are the paupers of state employees. I guess it's because the legislators figure our work should be its own reward."

Judd knit his brows. "So, what ever became of this loser? Is he still around?"

"Not around me, but he still lives in town—in a very large, and for this area, expensive apartment."

"Well, I hope his friends are properly impressed. But if you ask me, he's an idiot."

Karen giggled. "You don't even know him, so how can you say that?"

"Because he obviously didn't know when he had a good thing. He passed up the most attractive, sweetest woman in Silver Creek."

"I don't know about the attractive part."

"You don't? Surely you must know how gorgeous you are."

Karen just looked at him blankly. What could she

say? He seemed serious, but her slightly plump, farm-girl face and figure were obvious, for all the world to see.

"From the first time I saw you clearly, there in the diner the other afternoon, I thought you were one of the most stunning women I'd ever met."

Karen did balk at that—he must be exaggerating horribly.

"I love your eyes," he said, staring thoughtfully at her. "Even by moonlight, they're a beautiful sea green. I like the way they light up when you laugh. And your hair—" he stroked the curls around her face "—is the richest auburn I can imagine."

"You really think so?"

He chuckled. "Yes, of course. I'm glad you're not a skinny rake of a fashion model. Frankly women who look like they're starving turn me off. And those legs of yours. I swear, when you walked in the living room before dinner, I almost dropped the frying pan."

Karen threw back her head and laughed. At the sound, Judd's eyes darkened with desire. He moved closer and put his hands on her shoulders, drawing her near. Eagerly Karen accepted his kiss, opening her lips when he sought entry there.

"Mmm, you taste good," he murmured. He made it sound as though he'd been sampling a very fine wine, and the thought made Karen's heart thud even faster.

"So do you," she said as she welcomed him back to sample some more.

As though kissing her so thoroughly weren't enough, he deliberately spread his hands out over her upper back, the massaging pressure of his fingertips communicating his desire for her. His caress deeply aroused her, and she cried out in her mind for more, each touch of his hands, each stroke of his lips, fulfilling one craving even as he created another.

Then his hands slid down her back to the waistline of her shorts. Her spine tingled as his fingers played there, then reversed and slowly ran up her sides. Her back stiffened in a catlike stretch of anticipation, but he stopped the upward stroke just short of her breasts.

He feathered kisses from her mouth to the sensitive skin of her hairline, sending a shiver of pleasure down her neck and through her shoulders. When he cradled the back of her head and gently guided her cheek down to his shoulder, she nestled there and sighed.

But her bliss was soon shadowed by a creeping doubt. Her mystery man had taken her where she'd longed to go, but would she be able to keep him? Would some unexpected revelation in the days ahead make her regret her choice? Before her fears could ruin her happiness, she reminded herself that everything happened for a reason.

Meeting Judd hadn't been an accident, and she should have faith that everything would work out for the best. In fact, she was sure of it.

HALF A DOZEN official vehicles idled in a crabbed line along the verge of Wheeler Grade. Red-and-orange rotating lights stabbed into the inky sky, shooting weird shadows between the trees.

Half a mile into the forest, halogen lights with battery packs were strapped to the pines. The stark white light drained color from the faces of the uniformed deputies ringing the small clearing. One of them twisted away, another held a handkerchief to his face as he watched the two men with shovels. A German shepherd panted, strained forward and broke the circle of men, then whined and cowered back to its handler.

"Easy! That's enough."

Those with the spades gladly stumbled back, wiped sweat from their foreheads and moisture from their eyes.

A man in shirtsleeves and tie, carrying a black duffel and a flashlight, made his way through the trees.

"Coroner, over here."

"What have we got?"

"Woman in her late twenties, throat cut. Looks like she's only been in the ground a few days."

Chapter Seven

The two men wore suits, but they didn't look like salesmen, and it wasn't even nine o'clock in the morning yet. Karen removed her eye from the peephole and opened her front door.

"Miss Thomas? I'm Lieutenant Rossini, and this is Deputy Talmadge. We're from the Granite County Sheriff's Department. Is Mr. Judd Maxwell staying with you?"

"Yes, he's right here." She glanced over her shoulder down the hall to the living room. The bell had finally awakened her guest, who had declined to open up the sofa bed in favor of simply throwing a sheet and blanket over the cushions. Judd was sitting up, stretching on the couch. "Come in, please. I hope you have good news. How did you find out Judd was here?"

"Your office gave us his home address, and the apartment manager directed us here," the deputy said.

Judd stood up in his sweat shorts and T-shirt as she showed the men into the room and offered them coffee.

"No, thank you, ma'am," Rossini said. He shook

hands with Judd; the officer was of an age with Judd, but thinner, with pinched features and a sharp look. Rossini introduced his partner, a clean-cut blond fellow a few years his junior.

"You're detectives?" Judd said as the men took chairs and Karen and Judd sat on the rumpled sofa.

"Yes, we're with the investigations division of the sheriff's department. We'd like to ask you a few questions."

"Have you found the people who robbed Judd?"

Rossini pulled a pen from his inner jacket pocket. "No, I'm afraid we're still working on that. Now, Mr. Maxwell, can you tell us where you were headed on Highway 18 last Friday evening?" He began scribbling on a small pad.

"No. Unfortunately my memory still hasn't returned."

Rossini looked up from under his brows. "You have no recollection of the events of Friday night?"

"I have no recollection of the last thirty-three years, as far as my personal life is concerned."

"Since leaving the hospital, have you been able to reconstruct your movements last Friday?"

"To a certain extent, yes. Apparently I worked my afternoon shift at Summers' Chevron on North Main until five o'clock. I was gone from the station for two hours. Returning briefly, I spoke with my boss around seven. Where I went after that, I can't tell you."

"Can't?"

Though to all appearances Judd was calm, Karen could tell from his stilted answers that he was uncomfortable with the questioning. She jumped in to help him out. "We've been trying very hard to find out what happened to Judd, but it's difficult because he was new in town and didn't know many people.''

Rossini wrote on the pad.

''I have a feeling these questions aren't related to the theft of my belongings from my car,'' Judd said, looking directly at the lead detective.

Rossini matched his stare. ''That's correct, Mr. Maxwell. Actually we're investigating the murder of a young woman. Her body was found last night, in a shallow grave in the woods along Wheeler Grade. We don't have a final coroner's report, but it had been there approximately six days.''

''A murder! But that has nothing to do with Judd!''

Judd covered Karen's hand. ''They're talking to anyone who was spotted in the area the night the girl died,'' he explained in a low voice, then said to the investigators, ''I'm sorry, gentlemen, but there's nothing more I can tell you. My doctor, as I'm sure he'll inform you, believes my memory will return, but it will take some time. If at any point I remember something that could be helpful, I'll be sure to call you. Do you have a card?''

Both men handed him one.

''I'm sorry about the girl,'' Karen said. ''How, ah, how was she killed?''

Talmadge made a face. ''Her throat was cut.''

''How awful. Was she…?'' Karen wasn't sure she wanted to ask.

''Raped?'' Rossini said matter-of-factly. ''No, we don't think so.''

Karen shivered—the other was bad enough. They'd never had a murder so close to Silver Creek.

Wheeler Grade was miles down the highway, toward Granite City, but still...

The deputy raised his brows at Rossini, who nodded. "Thank you for your time, Miss Thomas, Mr. Maxwell. If we need to contact you, will you be here?"

"You'll have to ask Miss Thomas about that."

"Yes. Judd's looking for a new job in town." As soon as she said it, she wondered if she should have—the fact that he'd lost his job might make him look even more suspicious to these men. "He'll be staying with me probably until then." She reassured herself Judd's unemployment shouldn't make any difference; it wasn't like he was suspected of having anything to do with the killing.

"That is," Judd was saying, "if I don't wear out my welcome first." He grinned, and though it looked natural, Karen suspected he was acting for the officers. It made her vaguely uneasy. He continued to smile amiably as they all rose and shook hands again.

They followed the detectives to the door and watched as the men climbed into a white Taurus. It was obviously supposed to be an unmarked car, but the large aerial and the spotlight mounted on the front window frame stuck out. So did the government license plate.

Karen was about to close the door when an enormous, light blue Mercedes sedan pulled up in front.

"Oh, darn!" She was dying to discuss the police visit with Judd, and now it would have to wait. "It's my landlady and her husband. I hope they didn't see the car. I forgot they were coming over this morning."

"I think I'll get some coffee."

"Good idea." Karen didn't relish the idea of Mrs. Cohen, with her booming voice, being introduced to her houseguest on the front steps.

Karen wasn't sure if Judd would completely disappear, so she didn't mention him as she settled the Cohens in the living room. Mrs. Cohen was in full flight, describing her gardener's comic skirmish with the squirrels that had once again invaded the grounds of her family estate. The sleeves of her lime-green-and-lemon muumuu were flapping as she gesticulated, when Judd strolled in, cup in hand. Mrs. Cohen stopped abruptly, eyes popping.

"Hello there."

Karen was surprised the older woman didn't smack her brightly painted lips.

"Judd, I'd like you to meet Ruth and Truman Cohen. This is a friend of mine, Judd Maxwell."

"No introductions are necessary. We're already acquainted with Judd," Mrs. Cohen declared, grasping Judd's hand up to the wrist with her pudgy, jewel-studded fingers. "Though perhaps you don't remember."

Karen watched Judd briefly scrutinize the couple. They were of a height, the man being rather short, and both nearing fifty, but there Judd would find the resemblance ended. Karen rarely saw Truman, because he left the managing of his wife's rental properties completely up to her. But when the Cohens appeared together, Karen couldn't help thinking of them as a pair of birds, only with the sexes reversed. Corpulent Ruth was always clothed in brilliant colors and fantastic wigs, while her dapper spouse wore neutrals, tailored sport coats and sweater vests.

"I'm sorry," Judd said, "I don't recall your faces."

Truman nudged his wife aside, forcing her to give up Judd's hand as Truman extended his. "Truman Cohen. What my wife means is we heard about your unfortunate accident. I'm afraid news travels fast in Silver Creek."

"That's to be expected," Judd said. "You say we've met before?"

"Yes, at a play at the junior college, in Granite. What was it? *He Who Gets Slapped?*" Mrs. Cohen glanced at her husband, then continued before he could answer. "You were seated behind us, Judd, and we got talking at the intermission. We went for coffee afterward. It was a very enjoyable evening."

"I'm sorry, I can't recall it."

"It doesn't matter," Truman said.

"I rent this house from Mrs. Cohen. She owns my uncle's office downtown, too."

"They call me the Landlady of Silver Creek," Mrs. Cohen said. "Isn't that sweet? It's because I inherited so much property around town and own some of the principal businesses. My grandfather was one of the founders of Silver Creek."

"And Mr. Cohen," said Karen, "is an art historian, a very famous one, actually."

"In a certain circle," Truman said modestly.

"That's why we're here. I like to have Truman pick out the color schemes for my rentals once in a while. I tell him it's a chance to use his vast knowledge for a practical purpose." Mrs. Cohen chuckled at the tease, but she was obviously quite proud of her urbane spouse. "So, I'll let you get to it. I need to take the car down to Mrs. Pike's for just a moment, but I'll be right back. Please, Mr. Maxwell, don't say anything about yourself until I return, I want to hear everything!''

She departed in a flurry of floral draperies. Truman stuck one hand in the pocket of his neatly pressed trousers and with the other smoothed his little brown mustache. "I promise I'll get her away quickly when she returns."

"It's just that there's not a lot to tell her about Judd—"

"And if there were?" Truman said kindly. "Luckily Ruth didn't notice, she had her nose in her handbag as we drove up. But if Judd is staying here…" He glanced at the blanket and bed pillow on the sofa and paused a moment. Receiving no denial, he continued, "I'm afraid I must ask you, as my wife's tenant, if that was a police car which left your house as we arrived?"

"Yes." Karen sighed. She could tell him the detectives only came about trying to track Judd's robbers, but news of the murder would be all over town by the end of the day, and Truman would quickly put two and two together.

Judd spoke before she could. "There was a murder last week, somewhere outside town. Apparently the place where I was robbed and later found was nearby—they wanted to know if I remembered seeing anything that could be helpful."

"Judd was found on the highway, between Silver Creek and the Wheeler Grade turnoff," Karen added. "The girl was killed up on the grade somewhere."

"I understand." Truman nodded. "The people involved were probably from out of town, passing through. Still, it's dreadful. Quite natural the police would want to interview anyone who might have seen the girl and her attacker. No reason to mention it to my wife,'' he added under his breath, as though thinking out loud to himself, but Karen silently thanked him. ''Now—'' he clapped his hands to signal the subject closed ''—on to the mundane business of choosing paint for your walls. Have you any preferences, Karen?''

KAREN KNEW she would take more time picking the color of new underwear than she was spending choosing the paint for her home, but at the moment she didn't care. There were only two thoughts on her mind as she toured the cottage with Truman Cohen: finishing before Mrs. Cohen returned, and getting back to Judd, who had retired to the back sunporch with his coffee. Karen wasn't really sure which of the off-white and cheery yellow hues she was assenting to as Truman marked their names on a card with his fountain pen; the man spent half his time flying around the country, giving lectures on the great masters, so she figured she could trust him with flat and semigloss latex.

She had him on his way, out the door, within fifteen minutes, just as his wife returned and jumped from the driver's seat with amazing agility. Karen smiled as she closed the front door; she could hear the start of an argument, with Truman urging his wife to not make a fuss and come along quietly.

The smile quickly disappeared as she headed for the porch. The girl's murder was a dreadful thing. As she had listened to the detectives, for a nerve-numbing moment she'd wondered if Judd could be involved. But as her mind had begun to work properly, she'd realized that, of course, he had nothing to do with it. His car was found a long way from Wheeler Grade, and he'd been driving toward the grade turnoff, not away from it, as he would have been had he been fleeing the scene of the crime.

But the murder, while a tragedy in itself, could not have come at a worse time for Judd. Remembering the suspicions he'd expressed about himself two days ago at the bank, Karen worried he might now construe his gathering of funds Friday night as preparations to flee the police.

Karen paused in the porch doorway. The scene of their romantic tryst last night appeared far different in the midmorning light. They had kissed for only a few minutes before Judd whispered that it really was time they turn in. He'd been playing the part of the gentleman, she'd told herself, when she was feeling more like a wanton than her usual conservative, rather prim self. However, at the time she'd been too enthralled by the experience to feel any amazement at herself. She had lain awake in bed for some time, drowsy but delicious with the feel of his kiss still on her lips.

Now Judd, obviously deep in thought, was sitting in a deck chair with his back to her. Tanned legs and feet clad in zori stretched out before him. His calves and thighs were muscular and lean beneath their dusting of hair, bleached chestnut by the sun.

They're runner's legs, she thought.

Would the police blundering in this morning be a setback to their relationship? Judd might well tell her he'd decided, as he sat out here, that he couldn't remain her guest any longer. While she didn't like the idea of the whole town knowing Judd was staying here, now that Mrs. Cohen was sure to alert them, she had no intention of letting Judd fend for himself. It was time for a talk and some damage control.

She spoke. "Have you seen my cat this morning?"

Judd looked up from his reverie. "No, not since he streaked by me when I came in the front door yesterday."

"Poor Toby, he's awful with strangers." She took the chair across from Judd. "I'm not sure if he's afraid of them or simply offended by them. He refused to come inside practically the whole time my uncle stayed with me. I'll have to put some cat food out for him before I go."

"It's just as well if he's moved out temporarily, with my cockatiel in residence." Judd scratched at his bearded jaw. "I think I'll shave this off today. It's an itchy nuisance in this heat. I don't know why I didn't do it as soon as I left the hospital."

The thought of obliterating that handsome beard appalled her, but she stopped herself from blurting out an objection. "I suppose it isn't very comfortable. Is it going to be hot again today?"

"Not as bad as yesterday, in the low eighties, the weatherman says." He removed the morning newspaper from his lap and laid it on the table.

"Is there anything in the paper about the murder?"

"No, but I'm sure there will be by this afternoon. You all finished with the Cohens?"

"Uh-huh. Truman just left."

"I take it your landlady is a gossip?"

Karen nodded.

Judd sat up straight, then rested his right ankle on

his left knee. "I'm sorry if my staying here is going to cause a problem."

"No, no. Truman may well be able to convince Ruth to keep it to herself, and if he can't, well, it doesn't matter."

He accepted her assurance more quickly than she'd expected. "You should be on your way to your morning appointments, shouldn't you?" he asked. She had told him her schedule last night; on Fridays she always saw her Silver Creek clients in the morning, leaving the afternoon free for paperwork at home and thereby eliminating the need to drive in to her office in Granite.

"Yes, I have an appointment, but I thought you might want to talk before I leave."

Judd picked up his coffee cup. "About the sheriff's visit?" He downed the last swig.

"Yes. I really don't think you should concern yourself about it."

"Don't worry, I'm not. My car was stopped miles from where they must have found the girl, and the chances I saw anything that night are extremely remote."

"Uh, those were my thoughts exactly."

"Without a coroner's report, they've only got an approximate time of death. Rossini said 'about six days,' so she was probably taken up there and killed sometime Saturday, while I was lying in St. Mary's Hospital."

She'd been staring into the garden while he spoke, and she fancied his voice was slightly self-satisfied, almost as though he'd planned to be surrounded by witnesses at the time the girl died. She looked up quickly, noting his expression. *No, he's not congrat-*

ulatory, she thought. *Still, he's more at ease than I am, discussing the murder.*

A chill, like a little finger, poked at her spine.

"The fact she was buried in the ground may make it more difficult for them to ascertain the time of death, I imagine," Judd continued with a thoughtful frown.

The conversation was taking a strange turn. It wasn't that warm yet, but Karen felt damp beneath her arms. "I'm glad you figured all that out. I didn't realize you remembered the layout of the roads outside town."

"Oh, I don't," he said quickly. "The officers who picked me up later told me where I'd been found, and I looked the spot up on a map—there was one in the apartment."

"Oh." She didn't remember seeing any map when they'd searched his place, but it couldn't matter, could it? She suddenly felt anxious to be on her way. She stood, and Judd instantly rose, taking her hand as she stepped around him, then drawing her about to face him.

"I feel like getting out of here," he said. "You'll be back by noon—let's take a drive, see if any of the sights jog my memory."

"Okay," she said. Unlike the times before, his touch made her ill at ease. She dropped her gaze so he wouldn't know.

"You can do your paperwork tomorrow, hmm? And I'll start looking for a job."

What could she say?

"I'll do some cleaning up while you're gone."

The thought of him working around her house,

among her private possessions, was suddenly unsettling. She looked up. "There's really no need."

Her objection was useless; he just smiled indulgently. The lips that had given her so much pleasure last night seemed somehow thinner this morning, the upturned corners almost disconcerting beneath the cool gray of his eyes.

"Mmm, you look good today." Judd ran his hands over her bare arms. She was wearing a simple sleeveless cotton shirt and slacks. When she had dressed, she'd been disappointed that her more attractive clothes were all in the laundry. She knew she didn't look alluring. But Judd's eyes were turning from steel blue to indigo as he surveyed her. It was as if he wasn't seeing just her outfit, but what lay beneath it.

The knowledge of his arousal churned within her, seeking a reaction amid the confusion of her feelings. A whorl of answering desire overrode her apprehensions, her blood whispering how thrilling it would be to satisfy this virile male's curiosity.

His voice was a husky whisper as he told her, "When you get home, why don't you put on those sexy shorts you wore last night?"

"All right." She could feel herself becoming lost in the passion in his eyes. The pressure of his fingers on her arms increased, and he drew her to his chest. When their mouths met, a kind of energy leaped from him to her, electrifying her with the same sexual craving he'd infused in her last night. She wanted to jump into his arms, wrap herself around him. This gentle pressure of his lips wasn't enough! She desperately wanted to feel his tongue in her mouth, his hands exploring and melting her body.

Panic sounded in Karen's brain. Her feelings were too hot, too volatile and racing her out of control. She pushed back to try to save herself, tried to breathe and was relieved when he eased his hold on her. She didn't look at his face, afraid she'd see a knowing grin there. She mumbled something about being late and said goodbye, then went in search of her purse on legs that felt unsteady.

She couldn't relax even with the front door shut behind her. It had only been a parting kiss, very brief, yet she felt like she'd been shoved in a smelter and pulled back out again.

KAREN WAS TROUBLED, and confused, and very much in need of time to think. However, it would only take her ten minutes to cross town, and she'd have to deal with her first client, Mrs. Dempsey.

She was still shaking from Judd's kiss. She'd never realized how intense sexual attraction could be. And it had become clear to her as he kissed her how much Judd wanted her. Her stampeding hormones were making it almost impossible for her to think straight.

But she had to try, because something had not felt at all right about the things Judd said, and the way he acted, on the sunporch this morning. She had to recreate their conversation and forget about the embrace.

She'd grown comfortable with him over the past couple of days, felt she was getting to know him. And this morning he'd acted completely differently than she'd come to expect. He'd been like a stranger.

Perhaps she'd imagined it. Perhaps the problem was with her, not with Judd. Was she reacting to his

new calmness about his problems like a slighted
caregiver, being pouty that he wasn't leaning on her?
Was she reacting like a codependent when she should
instead be glad he was getting back on his feet emotionally?

But trying to figure it out was difficult when she
could still feel the sensation of him pulling her pos-
sessively to his chest, feel her will breaking inside
her like a slender branch in his hands.

She had to forget about that for a moment.... It
was so confusing. All kinds of thoughts had suddenly
started going through her mind as he talked about the
murdered girl in that nonchalant way. She'd even
wondered if he was hiding something, but she had
no reason to think that.

Or had she? What did she really know about Judd
Maxwell? He could be a drifter, perpetually under-
employed, or even unemployed, for all she knew. In
her rush to take care of him and champion him, had
she dismissed taking a more objective look at him?

If he kept kissing her like that, she'd never be able
to intelligently weigh the facts! She'd never, ever
reacted to a man this strongly. How could she think
of him dispassionately when she felt like selling her
soul every time he touched her?

Karen realized with a start she'd arrived at Mrs.
Dempsey's apartment. She couldn't remember driving there.

It was supposed to be a quick checkup on an elderly client who was doing quite well on her own
now. But, as she often did, Mrs. Dempsey wheeled
Karen into driving her somewhere when the local
seniors' shuttle could have done the same. Karen
tried with diligence to listen to her client as they

drove to Mrs. Dempsey's doctor's appointment, but her earlier anxieties about Judd were so strong, they were hard to put aside. Karen found it too easy to return to her own thoughts with both the radio tuned to Mrs. Dempsey's favorite news station and the lady herself chatting without a break. Karen knew her client enjoyed doing most of the talking and really didn't expect a response other than nods and one-word comments to show that Karen was paying attention.

Mrs. Dempsey was recounting the plot of *The Rockford Files* rerun she'd watched the night before when the radio announcer said, "The body of a young woman was found late yesterday afternoon by a local bird-watcher in the forest near Wheeler Grade Road, four miles west of Highway 18."

Mrs. Dempsey stopped speaking in midsentence and fixed on the radio. Karen turned up the sound.

"The Granite County Sheriff's Department has not been able to identify the victim, whom they describe as being in her late twenties. The body was buried in a makeshift grave some distance—"

"Appalling, absolutely appalling," Mrs. Dempsey said. Karen wanted to hear the rest of the report, but her client continued, "Young women are so foolish these days, getting involved with wife beaters and murderers! Surely it's obvious to the girls from the start what kind of men they're dealing with." Mrs. Dempsey took a rare pause and pursed her lips.

Karen's brow was troubled, and she didn't speak for a minute. "I wish I knew... No, I mean, you're right, of course."

HARD ROCK BLARED from the stereo as Karen let herself into her house. It was nearly loud enough in the

living room to make her cover her ears in self-
defense. She pictured the speakers exploding and
shooting sparks from the overload. She turned it
down a tad, but just so it was manageable. Judd was
her guest, after all, and she didn't want him to take
her lowering of the volume as a criticism. But she
couldn't help mumbling to herself, "How can he listen to this stuff?"

She herself only liked light rock, and some clas-
sical. How could Judd tune in to Billy Joel one day,
and the Head Bangers, or whoever they were, the
next? Where was he, anyway?

She called out his name above the music, but he
didn't answer. She could see the backyard through
the sunporch, but he wasn't outside or in the kitchen.
She hoped he wasn't using the only bathroom, off
the hall. She'd been perspiring in the car on the way
home, and she badly needed to splash some cool water on her face.

On the way, she passed the cockatiel's cage, and
noticed what she'd overlooked when she first came
in, that the big black cover was over the cage.

"Trouble?" she said. "Hey, Trouble." She'd been
in a daze at the time, but she remembered seeing
Judd remove the cover to feed the parrot when she
left this morning. There was no answering chirp from
inside the cage—poor bird had probably gone deaf
from the speakers only a few feet away.

Karen stepped into the vacant bathroom and was
instantly notified that Judd had been there before her.
A big navy plaid towel and its twin washcloth hung
to dry over the shower curtain rod. A brown leather
shaving kit sat at the back of the vanity. She remem-

bered Judd's elegant wooden toothbrush from his apartment, and wondered if it was tucked inside.

The pungent citrus smell of his cologne hung in the air. After breathing it a few moments, she felt dizzy, and told herself it must be the heat and lingering humidity from the shower. She turned on the sink tap full force and waited for the water to get cold.

It felt strange, seeing his precisely folded hand towel next to her faded pink one, jammed carelessly over the bar. Judd's elegant toiletries were incongruous next to the spotted water glass that held her lumpy tube of toothpaste and dime-store toothbrush.

It hadn't struck her until this moment how different Judd Maxwell was from her, how alien. She'd thought she instinctively understood him, that they were on the same wavelength, but how well could she expect to understand someone who spent money on luxury items without even bringing in a full-time salary?

To her working-class mind, such priorities were foolish, even wrongheaded.

She leaned over and splashed cold water on her face, then wiped the water from her eyes. Those beautiful towels had delighted her with their lush softness when she first used them in Judd's apartment. She reached out and hesitantly tested the terry cloth between thumb and forefinger. It still felt the same. Instinctively she reached for her own towel.

It was time to draw back, she decided. She'd jumped into a romantic relationship with Judd without really knowing who he was, and it had been a mistake to go so fast. She needed to wait until his memory came back, to find out who he really was, before deciding if it was wise to get close to him.

She looked in the mirror. A few hairs had come lose from her ponytail, and the style made her face look fuller. A *cuh-chug* sounded from the piping in the wall, startling her for a moment; it was the washing machine starting in the garage. Karen left her hair the way it was.

The familiar odor of automotive oil greeted her as she pushed open the connecting door to the garage. Judd was bent over at the waist, studying the dials on her clothes dryer. He'd changed into a fresh pair of khaki shorts and a body-clinging white tank top that drew Karen's eyes to his torso. His muscles were well-defined like a bodybuilder's, the skin tanned and smooth over the bulge of his biceps, triceps and the undulating contours of his back. His hair was slicked back and his face flushed, as though he'd been exercising. She vaguely remembered the weight training equipment from his apartment, and wondered if he had been using it today. Altogether he presented a picture of raw, powerful masculinity that was rather intimidating.

"Hi," she said. As he turned to her, she noticed the firm outline of his nipples beneath the thin cotton knit. She'd never been tempted to look at that part of a man's anatomy, but now she had to force herself not to stare. What was wrong with her?

"Hi." He adjusted a knob and pulled it out; the dryer started. He flashed her a smile of straight, strong teeth. "I didn't think you'd mind if I washed some of my stuff."

A pile of her own things sat on the washer where she'd dumped them this morning. A pair of her silky cream panties was clearly visible on the top, her pink cotton nightgown beneath it.

"No, ah, I don't mind at all," she said. He'd undoubtedly pressed her clothes down with his hands to get to the washer controls. With no one to see, she pictured him looking through her things, picking up her skimpy lingerie and running his fingers over the satiny fabric with a dark, hot look in his half-closed eyes.

The man was smiling at her. He didn't look the least bit uncomfortable that she knew he'd come in contact with her private things, as though it was understood between them he now had...rights over her.

Karen swallowed. She'd invited this intimacy; it was going to be harder to backpedal than she'd imagined. If she started holding him at arm's length, he'd surely notice and wonder why. And her years of training had taught her to never treat a client in any way that would hurt his feelings or undermine his well-being during a stressful period, unless she had an absolutely concrete reason for doing so.

She backed through the door, away from the scene of her dilemma, and he followed, telling her how he'd gone for a run and taken a look at the neighborhood.

Karen barely listened as they drifted into the living room. Without thinking, she reached out to pick at the cover of the cockatiel's cage.

"Don't do that!" Judd said. "He was driving me crazy this morning."

Karen jerked back her hand. "Was he being noisy?"

"I couldn't shut him up." He looked really annoyed.

Karen glanced doubtfully at the cover—the cocky little bird was absolutely silent now. It was getting warm in here, and it must be suffocating under that hood. "You said you wanted to go out—" she began, touching the cover again.

"No, leave it on." He caught her wrist. "I'm sorry. It's just, I think he's upset, being in a new place like this. It'll help calm him down if we leave him like that."

"All...all right." Judd had only grabbed her for a second, but an excess of emotion had fired in his eyes. Was it anger, at her, at the bird? Or fear? She bent close to the cage to pick a small gray feather from the carpet, and strained her ears for a flutter or some sound from inside. First her cat, Toby, had disappeared...

"I've made some sandwiches," he said. "Change into your shorts while I pack the car. I'd like to take a hike. The woods must be beautiful outside town."

Chapter Eight

Karen hugged the phone to her ear and prayed for her uncle to pick it up. Four rings…five. If Uncle Ed was out, why wasn't his answering machine coming on?

"Karen."

She jumped as a hand grasped her shoulder.

"Let's go, you can call your friend later."

"But I promised—"

"We'll be back soon, and I've waited all morning." He plucked the receiver from her hand and replaced it. Still grasping her shoulder, he steered her toward the front door.

She'd told herself she wouldn't go with him if she couldn't reach her uncle or another friend. She wanted Judd to know that someone was aware of his plans—as a kind of subtle insurance. But it was clear if she backed out now, there would be an argument with him, here in the house, where they were more alone than they would be out on the road.

As Judd helped her into his car, she tried to laugh off the doubts that had produced her growing fear, but she couldn't. Judd slid in beside her and pulled his sunglasses from the visor.

He drove smoothly with one hand, turning the wheel with a flattened palm at the first right turn, easing to a whisper-soft stop at the signs. From the clunky outward appearance of the old car, she had expected it to drive like a tank, but there were no rattles or squeaks, and she couldn't even hear the engine running.

Was the owner, like his car, far from what he appeared? From the corner of her eye, she saw that his face had gone blank. Casting back in her thoughts, she saw Judd impatient, and angry, and confused. But now the face, bisected by wraparound glasses, heavily bearded below, hair tight to his skull and gleaming above, was completely expressionless. It was impossible to tell if Judd was feeling pleasure, or pain, or nothingness. Looking for a sign of tension, she observed that even the cords in his muscular neck were still, almost as if he'd gone into a trance.

She squirmed as they neared downtown. If he turned onto Main Street, it would run right into the highway that would take them out of town.

"Judd." He didn't answer. "Judd."

"Yes."

"Why don't we go out to Silver Lake?"

"Which way is it?"

"Stay on this street and cross Main. I'll, ah, tell you when to turn."

She relaxed a bit as he followed her directions to the popular lake, out through the streets on the east side of town and past the old mill race. It was a short drive up a gravel road to the parking lot.

Judd easily pushed open the heavy driver's side door, but kept his right foot on the running board as he surveyed the view. Silver Lake sat in a crotch between the mountains, surrounded by steep, thickly forested slopes. A dirt fire road circled the water; it being late summer and the reservoir low, there was a gentle slope down to the surface of the lake. Men and women with fishing poles dotted the bank wherever a clump of trees afforded shade.

"There are a lot of people out here," he remarked.

"Yes," Karen said, feigning surprise. *As though she hadn't chosen this spot for just that reason.* Then, before he could suggest they drive elsewhere, she said, "Let's go," and started walking.

She made sure to keep a polite distance from him as they started around the lake. He wasn't walking fast, but she had to push herself to keep up with the ground-eating strides of his long, sinewy legs. She kept her hand occupied shading her eyes from the sun, but he made no move to take her hand or put his arm around her shoulders.

A pair of mountain bikers whizzed past them, shouting a conversation at one another. Then came a lone woman jogger wearing a headset. It was too hot. Karen wiped the sweat from her forehead with the back of her hand and wondered how anyone could exercise on a day like this without getting sunstroke.

Judd's ongoing silence was becoming unnerving. He didn't pause at any of the viewpoints or break his mechanical pace, ignoring the scenery and fresh air he'd claimed he wanted. What thoughts were brewing behind the passive face? she wondered. It was as though he'd withdrawn to some interior, secret war room where he was thinking, planning…what?

Or was her overwrought imagination making all this up? The thought brought a surge of relief, but she wasn't sure what to think. She'd probably feel terribly sheepish later, remembering how she'd gotten herself worked up over nothing!

She resolved to quiet her runaway fears by focusing instead on her physical senses. The air smelled of dust and algae, reminding her of the old rope swing and the summer afternoons she'd spent here as a child, fishing for crayfish with a string and a piece of hard salami. She tried to recreate the scene in her mind, but instead, the crazy thought flashed on her that this might be the last time she ever saw this familiar spot. Despite the heat, she shivered.

She had grown tired of shading her eyes and, without thinking, she'd lowered her arm. Judd unexpectedly moved closer, and before she knew what he was doing, he silently seized her hand. As though she'd grasped a tiger by the tail, Karen fancied she could feel the pent-up strength of every well-honed muscle in Judd's body.

His palm was strangely dry, the fingers cool, while Karen felt a film of perspiration everywhere on her own skin. They'd reached the far side of the lake, where no fishermen had bothered to venture. The rocky shore was deserted. She was afraid to move her hand in his; she wondered if it was trembling. She kept her eyes on the bank, feverishly telling herself she was being silly. An old severed fish head lay in the dust, a hook and broken line embedded in its jaw. Flies buzzed around it.

She had to speak, she couldn't stand it anymore. "You're awfully quiet."

"Just trying to enjoy the moment. Why don't you relax? There's a trail here, let's take it."

The foot trail he pointed to was a break in the trees and shrubbery, leading straight up the mountain.

"I'd rather—let's stay by the lake," she said, searching blindly for an excuse. "It's flatter."

"No, we'll get a better workout on the slope." He let go of her hand and gave her an encouraging push between the shoulder blades, up the trail ahead of him.

She had to move faster, or allow his hand to remain on her back. She didn't want that. She forged ahead, staying just out of his reach. The trail was narrow, the undergrowth dense on either side; there was nowhere to go but up. The warning sounds in her head were at full volume now—she knew it was a terrible mistake going up here with him, but he was quicker and in better shape than she was, and he was right behind her.

She wasn't used to this kind of exercise. Her breath started coming hard; she wondered how long she could keep going on this vertical grade. Twigs brushed against her bare legs, leaving scratches, but she dared not slacken the pace to see if she was bleeding. Ahead the winter rains had washed out the trail, leaving a rocky depression. She spotted a worn foothold and put her toe in it, grasped an exposed tree root to haul herself up, then Judd's hands were on her again, helping her the last bit of the way. She tried to get a few steps farther ahead of him as he negotiated the trouble spot behind her, but in two powerful steps he'd caught up with her.

The trail suddenly flattened and followed the contour of the mountain. Her thigh muscles gratefully relaxed and went rather numb. Her heart was pounding, and she noticed for the first time her throat had gone dry and parched. The trail widened slightly, and there was a view of the lake spread below them. The sun was shining on the water.

"You need a rest, let's stop here," Judd said.

Out of exhaustion more than obedience, she stepped off the trail, into the shade of the trees on the upside bank, then turned to face him. A lock of hair had fallen over his sweaty forehead, but he wasn't even breathing fast.

"This is a romantic spot, don't you think?" He looked around them, gesturing with widespread hands. His tone was strange, the movement, theatrical. "Yes, it's just perfect for what I want."

Karen felt the blood drain from her face and neck. He moved toward her, and she backed away. "What do you want?" she quavered, sure now she knew, afraid to hear the deadly answer.

Dark brows rose above his sunglasses. "Why, simply to be alone with you, of course."

Karen's back bumped against a hollow tree trunk. He'd been cool and collected when they started up the trail, but she could smell his masculine aroma now, see the wet stain on his tank top where his broad chest cleft in two.

"Isn't that what a man usually wants, when he's with a beautiful woman? A little privacy, to see if he can steal a kiss."

Was he gently teasing her, or mocking her? He braced an arm over her head, effectively caging her against the tree, and lowered his head to hers.

Even in the midst of her terror, Karen felt a thrumming, primeval pull in her chest, drawing her to him. Her inability to control her response to him excited her even as it increased her fear.

Slowly, inexorably he lowered his mouth to hers.

She kept from responding to him, but didn't try to pull away, either.

To her surprise, his kiss wasn't rough, but gentle; they were the lips she remembered from last night, tender and loving.

As she eased away from the tree trunk, he put his arms around her, the naked flesh of those incredibly virile biceps pressing against her own bare skin. Unable to resist, she moved her trembling hands to rest on his upper arms, felt the massive tautness of his muscles.

Judd continued lightly kissing her as he began to deftly rub her rib cage. The gently erotic message seemed to melt away her shyness and inhibitions. Like a feline stretching luxuriously at a post, she reached up around his neck and leaned into him. His palms softly kneaded the sides of her breasts through her T-shirt and bra, the probing thumbs finding and circling her awakened nipples through the lightweight fabric. A flame ignited inside her and burned down from her chest, through her belly, into the deepest, most womanly part of her.

But the voice of her fearful subconscious had not been completely silenced. It whimpered and whined beneath the surface, then broke through with words in her conscious mind. *This is madness! If he turns on you, you'll have no warning. Will you let him make love to you, and kill you?*

A pictured floated into her mind of herself lying half-clothed off the trail with her neck neatly broken, Detective Rossini saying, *Strange, there are no signs of a struggle.*

She withdrew her arms and squirmed to the side, the rough bark of the tree tearing at her top.

She was close enough now to discern his eyes behind the sunglasses. They'd been closed as he caressed her, but now he opened them. "What's wrong?"

Her receptive response to his embrace had one benefit; he wasn't suspicious yet.

If she acted naturally, didn't alert him to her fears, perhaps she could get away.

"I, ah, it's your beard. I'm sorry, but it's scratching my face something awful." She tried to look embarrassed, to smile apologetically. "You, ah, said you were going to shave it off this morning."

His left arm resumed its guard post over her head. Then he picked up a strand of her hair and rubbed it in his fingers. "I didn't get rid of the beard, because I knew how much you wanted me to keep it."

He was telling her he knew her thoughts! Karen's blood ran cold. Had he been sensing her emotions all day, planning to bring her to just this spot, because she knew he was the murderer? Before she had time to think anymore, he exploded.

"Don't tell me you don't want to kiss me because of the beard! I can read your mind, you see. You want me, but at the same time, you're scared to death. You've mulled everything over and decided I had something to do with killing Marlene Hall."

For a moment, the words hung in the air. Then Karen's eyes widened in shock. *The detectives had never mentioned the name of the murdered woman.*

Karen dodged under his arm and ran for her life.

"Karen!"

She flew back down the way they'd come, with no idea what she'd do when the level trail veered straight down the mountain.

"Karen, stop!"

The shout was ten feet behind her.

"I heard the girl's name on the radio this morning."

Karen slashed at the brush that reached out to slow her. He was gaining on her!

"I didn't mean to frighten you."

Karen saw the four-foot-long snake in the same second it saw her. It was crossing the sunny trail, and there was no way she could safely run around it or jump over it. The serpent instantly coiled its scaly body in the dust, its head up and back.

She stumbled and almost fell headlong as she fought to break her forward momentum. She was nearly on top of the snake when she stopped.

Karen stared in horror at the diamond-shaped head with its gleaming, malevolent eyes. There was a moment of silence, then the snake's pale, segmented tail began a fierce rattle.

"Oh, my God."

A sinewy black tongue flicked out and in, out and in.

"Karen, don't move."

She'd forgotten about Judd. His whisper was at her right shoulder. She stood frozen, unable to flinch if she'd tried.

There came a slight metallic clicking noise behind her, then Judd's arm jerked past her face and something silvery flew toward the snake.

The reptile's body reared backward, the knife catching it in the throat. Karen cried out as Judd pulled her back to safety.

"Don't look," he commanded, turning her to him and cradling her head. The rattling had stopped.

Karen gulped. "Is it…?"

"Yes, it's dead."

She let go a relieved sob. "I was sure it was going to get me."

"For a moment, there, I thought it was, too."

She could feel his heart pounding beneath her ear. She waited a minute, her arms reassuringly wrapped around him, as the congestion in her chest worked its way out.

When she looked up, he removed the offensive sunglasses that had made reading his expression so difficult. It was easy now to tell what he was feeling—deep concern.

"I hope you're not going to be upset I had a pocketknife on me," he said, searching her eyes. "I seem to remember some boyish target practice at a fence long ago, and most men carry one."

Karen brushed the tears and sweat from her face. "I'm not complaining, believe me. I'm just glad you've still got good aim."

"I'm sorry I startled you, coming out with the girl's name like that. The sheriff gave a press conference on the radio around noon and said they'd identified her. You were out on your appointments when it came on."

Karen struggled to think back. This morning seemed a week away. She'd left the Shensky sisters sometime after twelve. There had been no news of the murder on the radio as she drove home; the announcer must have just finished covering the story when she tuned in.

"I believe you," she said simply.

Karen waited while Judd quickly disposed of the snake carcass, then they went back to the lake the way they'd come. When they were on the flat again, Judd said, "Before we get back to the car, there's something I need to say to you." He gestured to a deserted bench with a view of the water and waited for Karen to sit down before joining her.

His bare eyes squinted in the sun as he stared at the lake for a moment before beginning. When he spoke, he didn't look at her, but his voice was full of emotion. "What I did just now, taking you up in the woods, was inexcusable. 'Sorry' doesn't begin to cover it, I know."

He sighed and shook his head.

"I've been in a strange mood all day. The detectives' visit this morning threw me, I guess. The run this morning didn't help, and I thought if we got out, away from town, that I could clear my mind, mentally relax and see if that didn't help some of my memories come to the surface."

"I noticed you were zoning out, but I didn't understand why."

"At the same time, almost without realizing it, I think I was testing you." Judd twisted his key ring penlight on and off between his fingers. "When we said goodbye this morning, you seemed upset, almost anxious. I wondered if you were having second thoughts about me, suspecting I was a murderer, and bringing you up to the lake was a way of testing your faith in me. However, by the time we headed up the mountain on that trail, I'd pretty much made up my mind how you felt. That's why I got so angry. Like I said, it was a rotten thing to do."

"Well, perhaps it was partly my fault." She explained how his unexpectedly even mood had thrown her off this morning and concluded by saying, "The facts of the crime showed you had nothing to do with it, so I shouldn't have let my imagination run away with me. Believe me, I don't have any doubts about you now." She thought, but didn't say, that if he'd wanted to do away with her, the snake's attack had been a perfect opportunity. He could have backed away from her and let nature take its course; he would have been accounted blameless when she died from the venom before reaching the hospital. Instead he had instantly come to her aid, and his quick thinking and coolness under pressure had saved her.

Small wonder then, Karen told herself, that even at this moment she was feeling a strong magnetic pull toward him. The memory of their kiss, up on the trail, flooded back. He had been so ardent but gentlemanly, only deepening the embrace when she made it clear she wanted him to...

Judd broke into her thoughts with a rueful chuckle. Apparently he was having his own, very different, reminiscences, for he rubbed his index finger over his lower lip and said, "I seem to spend half my time apologizing to you, and the other half terrifying you."

Karen couldn't resist a sudden urge to play the coquette. "Not always," she responded. Her lips pouted just a little as she regarded him through suggestively lowered lashes. Judd's serious expression turned into surprise and disbelief, then brightened into a grin of relief that was thoroughly charming.

Knowing she had the power to transform the mood of this moodiest, most self-possessed of men was amazingly gratifying. For the first time that day, Karen felt in control of her life again.

"Come along, Sir Maxwell," she said, rising from

the bench. "Enough dragon slaying and maiden saving for one day. Let's go home."

Judd put his right hand over his heart and inclined his head. "Whatever mi'lady desires."

Another rock on the back porch swing, perhaps? Karen thought. She gave him a queenly, albeit mischievous smile.

With alacrity, Judd fell into step beside her. The palm he placed on the middle of her back was at once respectful in its lightness, possessive in its heat. To Karen, it felt just perfect.

THE IMAGINATION WAS willing, but the body was weak. By the time they reached the house, emotional exhaustion had combined with lack of a good night's rest to leave Karen with only one desire: for sleep. When she sheepishly admitted she was dying for a nap, Judd looked sorry to part with her. But he graciously gave her a paternal peck on the forehead and told her to go get forty winks.

She paused long enough to say hello to Trouble as Judd removed the cover and took his pet out for a head scratch, then she went straight to her room.

When she awoke, the sun was going down, and she realized she'd slept almost three hours. She ran a wet towel over her face and torso and changed into a comfortable, ankle-length dress of turquoise knit.

Judd had voiced the intention of snoozing on the sofa, but she found him out back in the old rope hammock, reading a copy of *Stereo Review,* his trousered legs crossed at the ankle. He looked up as she came to stand next to him. "Have a nice nap?"

"Uh-huh." Karen yawned.

"Hungry?"

"Ravenous."

Judd rubbed his stomach through his striped sports shirt. "I hate to ask you to cook, but I've got a confession to make."

"What's that?"

"I think those fancy pots we found in my apartment were just for show. Those steaks I fried last night were pushing the envelope."

Karen smiled. "I've got a better idea. Since you saved my life this afternoon, let me buy you dinner."

On their way to the restaurant, Judd asked her preference before tuning the radio, and they talked about music for a bit. Karen felt relaxed, and Judd seemed to be enjoying himself, as well.

She suggested they eat Chinese food and Judd parked behind the downtown restaurant in a vacant lot. They held hands as they walked around to the front of the little building, talking about nothing and happy. Judd held the glass-fronted door open for her, and they waited beside an enormous fish tank as the proprietor rang up the bill for a couple in their early twenties.

The male customer sported a tight red T-shirt and blond crew cut. He worked a toothpick in his mouth as he put his change in his wallet, then looked up and did a double take at Judd. His lip slowly curled back, and his angry eyes never left Judd as he replaced the wallet in his jeans.

Karen knew there was going to be trouble.

Chapter Nine

"Do you know me?" Judd asked.

"No, and I don't want to, either."

"Curt. Curtis!" The young man's pretty girlfriend glanced uncertainly at Judd and Karen, then back at her sneering escort. She took his arm and tugged. "Like, we have to go, you know."

"All right, baby," he murmured, curling her arm protectively under his, but he looked as though he'd rather stay and spit on Judd than be led away.

"Whew," Karen breathed as the door closed behind them.

"I guess I must have forgotten to change his points," Judd said.

"What?"

"Unhappy customer."

"Oh, you mean a car tune-up. Do you remember him?"

"No, but he's not the first person who has recognized me, probably from the station. I told you it would get around town that the gas jockey from Summers' has amnesia. It happened once at the bank, and when I took that long run this morning. But everyone I asked said they knew me from the station and that was all. However, this is the first person who has shown any emotion other than friendly curiosity.''

''Well, he's welcome to keep his emotion until he finds a better one!'' Karen said it lightly, but the fellow's hostility had frightened her for a moment.

The slightly built young waiter, who had witnessed everything, flipped two menus in his hands and looked embarrassed. ''Very nice to see you, miss. I got a good table for you. Best. Please this way.'' He showed them to a quiet spot beneath a Chinese lantern, then made a small ceremony of pouring tea for them. When they thanked him, he flashed an enormous smile distinguished by a solid gold bicuspid.

When they were alone, Karen told Judd, ''The waiter is a nice fellow, I like him.''

''And not long in this country, from the thickness of his accent.''

''He and his twin brother are nephews of the owner. They came over from Hong Kong, I think, at the beginning of the summer.''

As they were discussing the menu, their host returned and set a hot plate between them. ''Pot sticker for you, on the house. You like to order now?''

''How sweet, thank you,'' Karen said, then let Judd order the dishes they'd decided on.

She was cautious about breaking the mood, but she hadn't brought up the subject since yesterday, and she couldn't wait forever to ask. When they had taken a few bites of the appetizer, she said, ''Did you see anything today that looked familiar?''

''I like the scenery around here very much, and the town seems somewhat familiar, but I haven't had any flashbacks to specific events. I still feel like I landed in Oz.''

He didn't seem disturbed she'd brought up the subject, so Karen continued, ''Do you think you used to fish or hunt?''

''I don't remember how to fish, the way I can remember details about old cars.''

''Considering how you felt about guns at my uncle's, you probably weren't a hunter, either.''

''Yes.'' He frowned. ''That was strange.''

She cupped her chin in her hand. ''Did you ski?''

''Hmm...I might very well have, though I don't think it was a passion. I doubt I came here for the recreation.'' He gave a rueful chuckle and leaned on the table toward her. ''There were a couple of old-timers, waiting in the bank teller's line behind me. The one said to the other, 'There's only three reasons for a soul to come to Silver Creek—to work in the mines, to retire or to hide from something.' I think he was talking about his new neighbor, whom he apparently didn't care for.''

''So you think you may have been running from something?'' Karen asked gently.

His expression was open and honest as he said, ''Not really. I don't feel I have anything to fear outside Silver Creek, though I suppose it's a possibility.''

His phrasing seemed rather odd, but she was too relieved he felt that way to question it. ''You lived in Los Angeles before, apparently. Do you remember anything about there?''

Judd rotated his water glass on the white tablecloth as he considered his answer. ''My only impressions of the big city are that it wasn't my favorite place. I don't know why, or how I know it, but I have this gut feeling I'm more comfortable here, out in the middle of nowhere, than I would be on a Los Angeles street. Perhaps I just got sick of urban life, and that's why I came here.''

''I think that would be perfectly understandable. I hate commuting to Granite City, but I'd rather do that than live there, even though it's not a large city by most standards. Ah, here's our dinner.''

As they ate, Judd asked her about her career. She told him how she'd worked as an intern during the summers before getting the full-time job in Granite, then described some of the more common problems she encountered in working with seniors.

Sometime during the meal, an older man came in and was seated across the room from them. After ordering, he occupied himself reading the afternoon paper. Karen didn't pay much attention to him, until her ears pricked up when the waiter asked him in a concerned voice, ''Everything all right?''

''Yes, it was fine. The paper, I hadn't heard—'' He glanced at Judd, saw he was being watched and cut off the sentence.

''I get you something else?''

''No, no, just this to go.''

The waiter carried two full plates of food back to the kitchen. After the patron hurriedly paid his bill and departed, Judd got up and scooped the man's abandoned newspaper from the table.

He unfolded it to the front page and scanned the headline. ''I was afraid of this.''

Karen put her fork down. ''What is it?''

''People are adding two and two together, and apparently I make four. In their minds, at least.'' His eyes flicked back and forth as he read.

"What is it?" Karen repeated.

"A story about the murdered girl. That man probably recognized me, like the others, and when he read about Marlene, he got worried he might be dining with a crazed killer."

"How ridiculous."

"Well, it's more reassuring to believe the murderer is a stranger than one of your fellow townsfolk."

Judd kept reading. "The county coroner released his preliminary report this afternoon. He's calculated the time of death as sometime between eight Friday night and one-thirty Saturday morning."

"Oh, no," Karen said in exasperation. The fact that the murder occurred before Judd was found on the road was sure to cause him more problems!

" 'The victim called the Creekside Diner in Silver Creek,' " he read, " 'where she worked as a waitress, around seven forty-five Friday night. Sheriff's officials say this is her last known contact with anyone before she was killed.' " Judd lowered the paper. "Isn't the Creekside Diner the place we stopped for lunch, the day you picked me up on the road?"

"Yes, it is."

"The older waitress was upset with our girl, the one who identified me, because one of the other waitresses was out." His brow furrowed. "I think she called the missing waitress Mar."

"You're right!"

"There's a little more." He read silently, then summarized, "Marlene lived out in the sticks somewhere, and the body was buried miles away. However, they think she was killed at her cottage and the perpetrator very carefully cleaned up after himself before transporting the body.''

Karen tried not to picture the murder scene, or the methodical killer mopping up all traces of his crime. It made her want to shiver, but she suppressed it. She kept quiet and toyed with her food as she let Judd reread the article. He took such a long time, she thought he must be memorizing it. When he finally folded the paper and laid it in his lap, she said, ''Would you like some more chow mein?''

His shoulders slumped. ''No, I'm finished.''

Karen surmised he hadn't counted on the murder taking place before he came down with amnesia, and discovering that the time of the killing could have coincided with his own accident must be playing havoc with his emotions. She wanted to talk to him about the story as soon as possible, but this obviously wasn't the place for it. She motioned for the waiter and asked for the check.

Neither of them spoke as they walked to the car in the lot behind the restaurant. It was almost nine; all the shops on Main Street were closed and traffic was light. A floodlight mounted on the back wall of the restaurant illuminated the parked vehicles. They were almost to Judd's car when a voice called out behind them.

''Hey, Maxwell, turn around!''

Karen gasped. There were four young men, with handkerchiefs covering their lower faces. The leader, in jeans and a red shirt, she recognized as the boy called Curt, who had scowled at them in the restaurant. The other three looked about the same age: late teens or early twenties.

"So," the leader demanded, "what makes you think you can pull into town, murder one of our women and get away with it by saying you can't remember?"

Judd's back stiffened, but his arms remained loosely by his sides. "You've got the wrong man."

"Oh, yeah?" Curt said. "You don't say." He held an iron golf club, which he beat lazily against his open palm. The boy next to him wore work gloves and brandished a two-by-four. The others carried fireplace pokers.

Curt stepped forward, and his pals fell into place beside him. "When we get done with you, you sicko, you won't remember who you are, *for real.*"

Karen glanced about desperately. Brick buildings surrounded them on three sides. The restaurant had a back door set in its wall, flanked by a garbage Dumpster, but the tough wielding the two-by-four had placed himself between her and Judd and the door.

Karen grabbed onto Judd, ready to step in front of him to stop the vigilantes from touching him.

"Karen, go!" Judd commanded, shaking her off. "No!"

"Go! I can handle this alone." His push propelled her several feet, toward the restaurant's back door.

"Yeah, lady," Curt said. "In case you didn't realize it, we're here to protect you. This guy is a killer."

She sent Judd a pleading look, warning him to be careful, then she ran for the door. The attackers grinned, obviously convinced they were doing her a favor and that she'd just woken up to it.

As she reached the door, there was a coarse shout

like a war cry. She turned to see the four vigilantes descend on Judd, weapons raised.

She ripped open the screen door and ran into her friend, the young waiter.

"Ah, wha—?" He dropped a bucket of vegetable trimmings between them.

"I'm sorry! I need to call the police. Where's your phone?" Her words ran together, and she was already past him, frantically searching the kitchen for a phone.

An elderly Chinese in apron and white cap was cleaning a giant wok with a brush. He discerned what she was looking for and gestured to a black phone on the wall.

She could barely hear the sounds of fighting over the loud rumble of the kitchen exhaust fan. She pictured Judd going down in a bloody pulp even as she gave the police dispatcher the address and begged her to have the cops hurry. She hung up and flew back to the door.

The owner was excitedly talking in Chinese to his nephew, who held the screen open, the better for the two of them to see. The nephew was jerking his body and shouting what sounded like encouragement. For a ghastly moment, Karen thought he was cheering on the four thugs.

"Ah, miss, you call police?" he asked as Karen crowded into the doorway next to them. "Those bad boys gonna go jail!"

The fight had moved to the middle of the lot. One attacker lay on the ground, cradling a twisted leg; his weapon was nowhere to be seen. The mercury-vapor floodlight bleached all color from the scene, casting the fighting figures in sepia tones. Without warning,

Curt rushed in from the side, swinging the golfing iron with all his strength.

"Oh, no." Karen couldn't bear to watch. She buried her eyes in her hands.

"You no worry about him, miss," the waiter said, kindly taking her arm, "your friend one bad dude. Look!"

Karen lowered her hands. Judd and his opponent were rolling on the ground, their two sets of fists locked on the club.

"This one know his stuff. You know, like kung fu. Judo. He *very* good."

The two men struggled to their feet, then shoved apart, the golf club remaining in Judd's grasp. With an arcing toss, Judd threw the weapon up onto the roof of the adjacent building.

Karen exhaled a tiny bit. "You mean he's been using karate or something?"

"Yeah, yeah." The two men nodded vigorously, and the younger one grinned. "He so good, he coulda break other ones if he try."

Her eyes stayed glued to the combatants, who were warily circling each other. "You mean he's been holding back?"

"Oh, yeah, he good enough break them for sure. He only try a..." He wrinkled his brow.

"You mean he's only defending himself? Not trying to hurt them back?"

"Yeah, yeah."

One of the other young men sprang forward. With a movement too fast to see, Judd grabbed the poker in one hand and the fellow's belt in the other. He rolled down and onto his back, propelling the attacker over him and jettisoning him into the back of a parked car. The boy's head just missed the bumper, but his shoulder crashed into the metal and he screamed.

After that, it was over in a matter of seconds. The injured one was helped from beneath the car by his friend, and the two of them half ran, half staggered out of the lot. The young man with the broken leg continued to moan on the ground. Curt, his bandanna mask hanging limply around his neck, faced off with Judd alone. However, with his buddies gone and no weapon in his hand, he wasn't so brave. He raised his fists before him and danced nervously from foot to foot.

Judd was breathing hard, and a thin stream of blood ran from his mouth. He watched the young man in front of him as he wiped his lips with the back of his hand. "Quit while you're ahead, kid."

The wail of a distant siren made up Curt's mind for him. He turned and fled the scene without a backward glance. Karen cried out and rushed forward to hug Judd.

Two patrol cars pulled into the parking lot. The officer from the first knelt by the injured boy, while the second hurried up to Judd and Karen. "What's going on here?"

"Nothing," Judd said, dabbing his lip with a folded handkerchief. There was a tear in his shirt, and his slacks were streaked with motor oil and dirt. "Just a mutual disagreement that got out of hand."

"Disagreement?" Karen exclaimed. "There were four of them, wearing masks. They jumped Judd for no reason."

"What's your name?" the officer asked.

"Maxwell. Judd Maxwell."

The cop's brows went up. "The guy with the memory loss?"

"That's me."

The officer seemed nonplussed, and excused himself to check on the hurt boy.

"Are you all right?" Karen asked. .

"Yes, it's nothing. I just cut the inside of my lip."

The officer returned. "The kid's leg is pretty bad, but he admits he started it—otherwise, I'd have to detain you."

"You mean arrest him?" Karen was furious. "But *they* attacked Judd."

"Karen, let it go," Judd said.

"But don't you want to file a complaint? We can identify the leader."

"It doesn't matter. Are we free to go, Officer?"

The cop hesitated. "I'll need some information for an incident report, then you can leave."

Karen gave her name and address as an ambulance arrived. The cop moved his car so Judd could back his out.

As they drove home, Karen said, "I don't understand why you didn't want to prosecute those troublemakers."

"Maybe it's because I understand how they felt," Judd said. "After all, this is their town, and I'm the mysterious outsider in it."

"I think you're being too forgiving." She sat back sulkily. After a few moments, she said, "You did pretty good back there. The men from the restaurant seemed to think you were some kind of black belt."

"I'm very tired, Karen" was all he said. "Let's talk about it in the morning."

JUDD AWOKE the next morning in a panic. He swallowed the shout that had started in his throat and held his breath as the nightmare slowly faded. It was then he realized he wasn't on Karen's couch, but lying in the hammock in her backyard.

"Damn." His stomach remained in knots as he eased himself to a sitting position and rubbed the dew from his face. He hadn't realized before that he was a sleepwalker, but now, somehow, he knew it was true. It was the reason he now found himself out of doors when he'd begun the night under a blanket in the living room.

For the first time, he remembered his dreams, and he wished he didn't.

He wished he could forget the three women, young and pretty, their bodies horribly mutilated with deep slashes.

He checked his hands, front and back, for cuts or blood. They were a little blue from the cold; that was all. It was freezing out here. He freed himself from the hammock and went inside.

Though his memory hadn't returned, he was learning a lot about himself, none of it comforting. He knew how to use a gun, how to keep cool when attacked, how to fend off other men with a form of martial arts that smacked more of back alleys than a controlled judo hall. And if his dreams held any meaning, he might know how to inflict terrible pain and how to kill without mercy.

Judd shivered as he stepped into a steaming shower. He was clearly more than a simple car mechanic. But what? The skills he possessed were those of the mobster, the youthful gang member, or someone who had survived the criminal teaching ground of prison. Had he been a cold war spy, a mercenary or a hired assassin even? Those explanations all seemed too far out to be true. As impossible as his dreams were horrible. If the pieces didn't start fitting together soon, he would go mad with the uncertainty!

Karen was still asleep behind her bedroom door as he mechanically uncovered and fed Trouble. He made the coffee extra strong, then brought in the morning newspaper.

He recognized the big black-and-white photo even before the front page was completely unfolded, and his heart stopped. It was one of the women from his dream. It was Marlene Hall.

Chapter Ten

Karen woke at her usual time, a few minutes before seven. She changed out of her nightgown into a turquoise sweat suit, then opened her bedroom drapes. It was a gray, overcast morning. If she wasn't mistaken, the heat wave was over, thank goodness. She wasn't even going to entertain the possibility that the gray sky could turn to thundershowers sometime today.

She found Judd in the living room, fully dressed in slacks and a white dress shirt. He was hurriedly stuffing something into his suitcase. The thought he was packing to leave struck her like a blow.

She swallowed, instinctively realizing that the best way to lose him would be to hold on too tightly.

"You're up early," she said breezily. "You look nice. Are you going job hunting?"

He straightened, hands on his narrow hips. "Good morning. No, I'm not going job hunting." His gaze slid to the coffee table, then returned to her face. "I need to have a talk with you."

He ushered her to the dining table with an outstretched arm that did not touch her. She was very aware that their last physical contact had been yesterday evening, just before they entered the restaurant. He hadn't touched her since learning of the time of Marlene Hall's death, during dinner, and Karen felt sure it wasn't a coincidence.

"I made some coffee. Would you like some?" he said as she sat down.

"Yes, thanks."

He came back with a single cup, then took the chair on the opposite side of the table from her, rather than in his usual spot catercorner from her.

"I don't want to upset you," he said gravely, "but I'm going to the Creekside Diner this morning...to talk to the people Marlene Hall worked with." A tortured look appeared in his eyes. "I need to find out how well I knew Marlene."

The thought of putting anything in her stomach suddenly appalled her; Karen carefully pushed her cup aside. "I see." She felt scared and angry at the same time, but mostly angry at this new threat to Judd's peace of mind. She tried to keep the impatience from her voice as she said, "Do you have any reason to think you were acquainted with Marlene, other than the fact that you used to eat there sometimes?"

Judd's gaze slid away. "Not really."

Karen was too preoccupied to notice the edge of guilt in his tone. Her intuition was shouting that if she let him leave, he might never come back again. "Do you think it's wise for you to go out today, after last night? Perhaps it would be safer to lay low for a while?"

Judd straightened. "I won't be in any danger. There may be a few calls to the mayor demanding my arrest, but I don't think anyone else will try to take the law into their own hands.''

Not after the drubbing you gave those four hot-shots, she thought, and smiled despite herself.

Apparently he thought she wasn't taking the subject seriously enough, because he frowned. ''Karen, I have to level with you. I've had a strong gut feeling, ever since I woke up in St. Mary's a week ago, that I was in some kind of trouble. I left the hospital because I felt it was imperative I find out who I was and what I'd been involved in, before something worse happened.''

''That's why you tried so hard to get rid of me? Because you didn't want me to get involved in whatever it was?''

''Exactly. Day before yesterday, when you told me my feelings were perfectly normal, that the anxiety was merely a symptom of the amnesia, I began to relax and tell myself I had nothing to worry about. Then yesterday, when the cops came to talk to me, I convinced myself it was all a coincidence. All day I kept denying I could be involved in the murder. Well, I was fooling myself.''

She watched as his mouth compressed into a bitter line, and she realized his words had been full of recrimination at what he must consider his own gullibility. His behavior over the past days suddenly made sense to her. He'd been going through the grieving process of a person with a serious illness, first angry at the loss of his memory, then denying anything was wrong! Why hadn't she immediately recognized the classic behavior pattern for what it was? And now he was calm, coming to terms with what he believed to be the truth. Unfortunately he'd drawn a terribly false conclusion. He wasn't accepting the fact he had a temporary mental disorder, but that he was a murderer!

"Trusting your feelings at this point could be a big mistake—" she began.

"Karen." He thrust one arm forward, palm up. "Whether I held the knife or not, I'm in deeper than I thought. Most of the town is probably convinced I'm guilty. I'm the prime suspect. You know the police will be back. I need to know what to tell them when they come—I've already wasted too much time when I could have been searching for the truth."

Karen thought quickly. Knowing Granite County, she had to admit he was probably right about both the townsfolk and the authorities. If he was seen to be investigating the murder himself, it might lend more credibility to his amnesia claim. And going to the coffee shop would serve a further purpose: it would prove to Judd that he hadn't been friends with Marlene, that she was just another waitress. It would relieve his mind.

She took a sip of her cooling coffee. "Maybe we should visit the diner. I'll get my clothes on and we can go."

"There's no need for you to come with me," he said as she rose.

She circled the table and put her arms around his neck from the back. "Do you want the truth, or do you want to be Rambo?"

He snorted, and she sensed her touch was softening his resolve. The thought thrilled her that she could influence such a forceful, determined man.

"Then take me with you," she whispered, her

mouth close to his ear. "I know my way around town, and I can help."

It was just enough manipulation; she didn't want to overplay it or he'd insist on reasserting total control and leaving her out. She drew away with a last squeeze to his shoulders and went to dress before he could change his mind.

THE ENVELOPE WAS STUCK to the front door with tape. As she removed it, Karen glanced back into the hallway; Judd was still searching the house for his misplaced car keys. With a sense of foreboding, she drew out the single sheet of typing paper. A short message was printed neatly in block letters.

I HAVE EVIDENCE THAT JUDD MAXWELL
KILLED MARLENE HALL.

A FRIEND

Karen harrumphed in disgust and started to tear the letter in two, but Judd was approaching. She stuffed the paper in her purse.

She didn't want to think about the note, but after she'd straightened out her conservative, beige shirt-dress and wrapped her long raincoat around her legs for warmth, there was little else to distract her on the silent ride to the Creekside Diner. Judd was deep in thought, his eyes scanning the mist-shrouded road without really seeing it.

Some friend, she mused, to send her a poison-pen letter like that! If the author had truly had her best interest at heart, he or she would have called her on the phone, told her up front what the author purported to know. It was obviously a prank, an adolescent trick, and one in very poor taste.

It bothered her that she couldn't think who would have played the joke. The thought crossed her mind it might have been her old boyfriend, Mark the engineer, but that was ridiculous. She might have jilted Mark, even possibly wounded him when she turned down his proposal of marriage, but she doubted it. Mark was too focused on his goals, too sure of his ultimate success in life to let a little thing like being turned down by Karen Thomas get to him.

They found the diner's tiny parking lot full when they arrived. Judd pulled past and parked on the verge of the highway. As they walked back to the restaurant, Karen admired Judd. He looked even more handsome than usual, dressed up in a striped tie and tweed sport coat, minus the ubiquitous sunglasses.

When he opened the entrance door for her, the heavy aromas of frying bacon and sausage, mixed with the sweet smell of maple syrup, assailed her. Judd took a quick look around the dining room, then headed toward a slim waitress with a lion's mane of blond hair who was pouring coffee and wisecracking with a customer. Karen recognized her as the mature woman who'd been working the shift with Allison, the girl who recognized Judd.

"Ricky," the balding customer said as they approached, "you shouldn't tease me."

"I'm not teasing you, I like your hair. It's the nicest one I've ever seen."

The customer threw back his head and guffawed; Ricky's shoulders shook.

"Miss, I wonder if we might have a word with you," Judd said.

Ricky turned, a Cheshire grin on her brightly painted lips. The smile disappeared as she instantly recognized Judd, and her eyes widened for a second.

"What in the hell are you doing here?" she growled, teeth nearly clenched. "I thought they'd 'a locked you up by now."

"I need to talk to you for a few minutes."

The waitress laid a hand on Karen's arm and quickly ushered them through a swinging door into the kitchen. "There's the back door, now use it!"

The big, dough-bodied cook turned from the grill and started. The waitress Allison had been slicing oranges at the cutting board. When she saw Judd, she let out a little cry. "Lenny, it's him." Karen had to step aside as the girl scuttled into the dining room.

"Please," Karen said, deeply guilty at the disturbance they were causing, "we just wanted to ask you a few questions. It will only take a minute."

"We all made statements to the police," Ricky said, hands on her hips. She was probably in her fifties, but her faded jeans fit like leggings, and an inch of shiny gold bangles jangled on her left arm. Karen thought she resembled nothing so much as an older, but still exotic, mountain lioness. "You got any questions, you ask the cops."

The cook picked up a cleaver and held it at the ready.

"We're sorry we bothered you," Judd said. Karen followed him out the back door and as he strode quickly toward his car.

"Damn." He hit his leg with the palm of his hand.

"It's going to be impossible to learn anything if everyone's already tried me."

Hating to see him discouraged, Karen automatically said something positive. "Maybe not."

"Come on, honey! What else do you expect me to do? Walk into the sheriff's office and ask them politely if I can see my file?"

"No, of course not." Karen thought a moment. "Perhaps, if I go back alone, the waitresses will talk to me."

Judd leaned a straightened arm against the hood of his car. "I don't want to ask you to do that."

"You're not asking, I'm volunteering. I came along to help, remember?"

Conflicting desires warred in Judd's face. Finally he said, "All right. I don't suppose they'd throw a defenseless woman out on her rear, but that cook looks a little crazed. Be careful."

Karen wanted to point out it was Judd's presence, not her own, that seemed to raise Lenny's blood pressure, but she refrained. "Don't worry. I'll be back in a minute."

The heat and humidity of the kitchen enveloped her as Karen stepped through the back door. Ricky had her arm around Allison, who had obviously been crying. Guilt washed over Karen again, but she pushed it aside and put on her most humble, nonthreatening smile, the one she used when visiting elderly clients in their homes for the first time. It said, *Thank you for seeing me, and please excuse me for invading your space.*

"Ladies, I'm sorry. If you could, please, it really would help me out if you talked to me for just a minute."

Ricky exhaled, ruffling her bangs, then seemed to make a decision. "Allison, you go wash up." She patted the girl's fanny. "And get back out there pronto before they start climbing over the counter."

Allison avoided Karen's gaze as she blew her nose and obediently left. Lenny glanced apprehensively from where he was frying up some hash browns and eggs, but he seemed to be calmer now that Judd was gone.

"We were all real fond of Marlene," Ricky said stiffly, crossing her arms over her chest. "You can imagine how hard this has hit us. Allison especially. And I've got to be out there, forcing myself to kid with the customers like nothing happened. We may look fairly busy this morning, but they're usually waiting out the door on Saturdays. If folks are made to feel any more jittery than they already are, we'll never get 'em back."

"It must be very difficult for you, and I'm sorry, really. I know it was a shock to you seeing Judd here. I'm a social worker for the county, you see, and I've been assigned to help him until he recovers his memory. Did you, ah, know he has amnesia?"

Ricky sniffed. "Yeah, I heard some rumor to that effect."

Karen cut to the chase. "It would be a great help if you can tell me how well Marlene knew Judd."

"I'll tell you exactly what happened, straight. Marlene had a date with a man the night she was killed—she and Allison were working the lunch shift and Marlene told her. That evening, Mar called here close to eight o'clock. I answered the phone. She told me she was going out of town for a week or two."

Ricky paused, and the back of Karen's neck prickled. She thought of Judd arriving at Summers' Chevron at seven the same night and demanding his back pay, not appearing to care when Howie told him to never come back.

Ricky cleared her throat and stared at the floor. "Mar was embarrassed asking me to cover for her with the boss lady—she'd never done that before, played hooky I mean—but she sounded happy about the trip. Me and Allison were sure she was going away with the guy." The older woman looked up and fixed Karen with eyes that were cold with anger and grief. "We figure now that the murderer led her along so she'd tell everyone she was going out of town and we wouldn't get suspicious and start looking for her right away. Heck, if they hadn't found her body, Allison and me probably would have assumed she'd eloped and just decided not to come back."

"Did she, ah, tell you her boyfriend's name?"

"No way. Mar was very private and never talked much about her men, so we can't prove it was Judd, but we took a kind of poll, and Allison was sure it was Judd Maxwell. He's smooth and so sincere, you know. Just the kind of guy who could lie his way barefaced into a girl's heart, never let her know what he was really like until he turned on her."

Thoughts were beginning to whirl much too fast inside Karen's head, making it hard for her to form her next question. She tried to slow down, to focus for a moment on the sounds of clinking cutlery and rustling newspapers that blended with the hum of conversation from the other room. Ricky's estimation of Judd's character could be pure imagination. But standing here, speaking with Marlene's friends, was making the murder too real, whereas before it had been just a grisly story someone told her. She mustn't convict Judd on circumstantial evidence, on what might be coincidence.

Karen took a breath. "What made you think Judd was, ah, was Marlene's lover?"

Ricky leaned back against a freezer and crossed her arms. "Judd was friendly with all the waitresses, but especially Marlene. He used to come in here four or five times a week, for an early lunch, and he almost always sat in Mar's section."

Karen tried to think of reasons, other than the obvious one, why Judd would have driven clear across town and beyond the city limits to lunch at the diner. It *could* be because he liked the food, and because the friendly atmosphere made him feel he wasn't eating alone.

She made herself ask, "Did Judd flirt with her?"

"No." Ricky shook her blond mane. "He didn't flirt, just talked to her. But sometimes he'd tell her something funny and she'd laugh—and he didn't joke that often with the rest of us. And he left Mar big tips. He didn't come on to her, though. That wouldn't have been the right approach with a girl like Marlene."

"What do you mean?"

"Well, Mar wasn't really the sort you'd expect to find waiting tables for a living. She had more class, and not the same kind of interests as most folks. I always wondered why she hadn't gone to college, maybe got in a fight with her parents, and that's why she left home. She was only twenty-four or -five, and she wasn't from around here."

A voice called from the counter on the other side

of the pass-through, "Hey, Ricky, you ever comin' out? I can see my breakfast gettin' cold up there."

Ricky glanced fretfully over her shoulder, then stepped toward Karen and focused hard on her. "Sweetie, if I were you, I'd get as far as I could from that character and hide myself. I don't care if he's your job or you're stuck on him, or whatever—it's not worth it. I'd bet my life that this guy killed Marlene just for the fun of it. She was a sweet young girl, just like you, and she'd never do anything to make a man slit her throat. This jerk got his kicks gaining her trust and then doing her in, and you can bet it's not the first time. He's probably left a string of redheaded dead women across this state."

"Red?" Karen reached reflexively to touch one of her curls. "Marlene had red hair?"

"Yeah, sweetie, long and wavy. A lot like yours." Ricky plucked the morning paper off a shelf next to a radio and showed Karen the front page. "See. The picture's black and white, but the two of you could be cousins—or sisters."

Chapter Eleven

It was a fatal mistake to leave by the diner's back door.

But it was too late. Still reeling from what Ricky had told her, she'd left the kitchen the way she came in. Now, as Judd rushed toward her, she wished she'd thought to call a cab or find some other way to get back to Silver Creek on her own. It seemed just possible now that Judd had killed Marlene. Perhaps he'd blacked out before he did it. Perhaps he had a split personality or something. She simply didn't know.

"You were in there a long time," he said, a strange look of relief on his face.

"Not really." She couldn't tell him what Ricky had revealed. She had to pretend.

"Are you all right?" He was trying to catch her eyes, his hand hovering near her arm but not touching it. There was almost a quaver in his voice as he asked, "What did they tell you?"

"Nothing, really." Karen walked fast to keep ahead of him, to keep him from seeing the distress in her face. "They, ah, they were too busy to talk, I'm afraid. The cook let me wait in the kitchen for a few minutes, but the waitresses couldn't get away, or wouldn't.'' Feeling sick inside, she flashed him a smile over her shoulder that she hoped conveyed apologetic frustration.

"I'm sorry it was a wild-goose chase.'' He followed her closely around to her side of the car. As he unlocked the door for her, caution warned her not to get in. She waited for him to step away, wishing desperately that some more believable excuse would come to her before she was forced to speak, but it didn't.

"Would you, ah, would you mind if I stayed and got some breakfast? I'm really hungry—''

"Here?''

"Yes, I think I'd rather not wait. You don't have to stay if you've got, ah, other things to do. I'm sure my uncle will give me a ride home if I call him.''

He was frowning. He obviously knew something was up. He'd never let her go now!

"I've got a better idea.'' He was suddenly smiling, the instant congeniality ominous. "Why don't we drive into Granite City? Maybe there we can find a place where everyone won't recognize me off the bat.''

Before she could protest, he pulled open her door. "Come on.''

Karen craned her neck to watch as he circled the car. She could jump out and make a run for it, but they were yards from the diner parking lot, and there wasn't a soul in sight. If he sprinted after her, he could catch her and drag her back to the car without the coffee-shop patrons ever spotting them.

She weighed her chances for safety as he slid in beside her; it was a long drive to the county seat, and traffic on the two-lane highway would be light on an early Saturday morning. "I'd rather not go to Granite," she said, at the same time lying to herself, telling herself she had nothing to worry about. The mental ruse began to work, and she added more calmly, "I make that drive every day, you know. We can go back to my place, and I'll fix us something."

He threw her a questioning look, then started the engine. "That would be fine, if you don't mind."

"Yes, let's go back to the house."

Judd wheeled the car around and applied his foot to the accelerator, setting his course back to Silver Creek. Karen sat rigidly beside him. He couldn't really imagine honest Karen lying to him about the waitresses not talking to her, but something had spooked her badly. He'd felt tension flowing from her the moment she stepped from the diner.

Judd rubbed his chest, which was strangely tight.

How alive he felt to Karen, how attuned to every signal of her emotions! All morning, since seeing Marlene's photo in the paper, he'd felt oddly detached from his surroundings, as though he were an objective observer watching Judd and Karen investigate a crime that involved someone else. Only when he'd witnessed her distress had a part of him begun to feel again.

His feelings for her obviously ran deeper than his own sense of self-preservation. Time was of the essence, yet he'd suddenly judged it more important to take her into Granite if it would have relieved her distress.

But normal, pleasant diversions like weekend drives weren't meant for him and Karen. He couldn't escape reality, and he'd been dreaming to think for a moment it might be possible.

As he drove, Judd struggled to find something to say to make her less afraid of him. But what could he say that wouldn't smack of outright hypocrisy, what assurances could he give about himself that weren't potential lies? Karen Thomas was probably wise to be frightened of him. As they neared town, he forced himself to accept the truth: allowing Karen to go on being afraid of him was probably the kindest thing he could do for her. And at that moment, he felt a part of himself die.

The silence made Karen nervous, but it was easier than trying to talk and act as though nothing was wrong. They had just entered town when she spied a man on the sidewalk a block ahead, waiting to cross the street at Silver Creek's first stoplight. She thought she recognized the figure. Yes, it was her uncle Ed, and the light was yellow. It must be a sign from heaven. She wasn't sure Judd was guilty, and bailing out on him would be like taking sides, but this was her chance, and she knew she had to grab it.

Ed saw her through the windshield as Judd slowed the car for the light. He squinted, then raised his hand in a wave. As they came to a stop behind another car, Karen said, "There's my uncle. I'd like to talk to him."

She shoved open the door and scrambled out to safety.

Ed Thomas came toward her with a smile that mixed pleasure with surprise. "Gee, you're anxious to see me," he said.

Flushed with relief in Ed's familiar, comforting presence, she threw her arms around him and squeezed tightly.

"Are you okay, pumpkin?"

"It's Judd," Karen said shakily while trying to keep her voice down. "We were just at the Creekside Diner, and I had a talk with the head waitress."

"Ricky Black, you mean? That woman's got a big mouth and an imagination to match. I had a chat with her myself last night."

"You did?"

"Sure. I tried to call you at the house, but you must have been out and I didn't leave a message. I've got some news for your client."

Judd had swung the car around the corner and parked. He approached them now and held out his hand to shake Ed's.

"Morning, Judd. I was going to phone you later. I've got some information for you."

Karen suddenly remembered that she'd forgotten to tell Judd she had gone over his head and asked her uncle to check into his background. However, Judd appeared neither angry nor worried by her uncle's words, just a little surprised perhaps. She remembered what Ricky had said about Judd being smooth and adept at dissembling.

Ed added with enthusiasm, "I located your ex-wife, Judd. Cynthia Peltz was her maiden name. She's still living down in Irvine, where you were an undergraduate at the University of California. She said she was a part-time student and worked in a sandwich shop near the campus, where you two met. But perhaps you'd rather talk later, in my office, and I can tell you the rest."

It was a bit windy on the street, but there was little traffic and no pedestrians. Judd's eyes were burning, his total attention focused on the private investigator.

"No, please go on," he urged, and ushered the three of them into the protected alcove of a closed-up shop.

"Well, Cynthia claims she was unsure about the marriage from the start, but you were very much in love with her and talked her into it. Anyway, it didn't last long. There were no children. I tried to get information about your family, but her memories were too vague to be of any use. She hasn't seen or heard anything from you since the divorce.

"I asked her about the breakup, thought it might help you remember. She described you as being 'uptight and puritanical,' but reading between the lines I'd say you probably preferred studying or taking in a movie while she wanted to barhop." He gave a sorry shake of his head. "Anyway, you split up after only a year and a half, she filed for a divorce and she remarried immediately after the papers came through. Something she let slip confirmed she'd met the other guy while you two were still together. Apparently you took the whole thing rather well, because even though her memories of you aren't real fond, she couldn't come up with anything bad to say about you."

Ed paused a moment to allow the information to sink in. Her uncle's news, combined with his friendly, trusting demeanor with Judd, was easing Karen's fears. Her limbs felt rather limp after the sustained charge of adrenaline, and she was beginning to feel a little foolish.

"Did Cynthia know if I'd ever remarried?"

"No, she didn't, but I'd say the chances are extremely slim. A former associate of mine now works for a big investigation firm in Tampa that has a database of marriage and divorce records you wouldn't believe. That's how I found Cynthia.''

''I see,'' Judd said. Karen thought he looked relieved. ''I appreciate you doing this for me, sir, and I want to pay you back. Is there any more?''

''Yes. I contacted your academic advisor at Irvine. He said you were a history major and you enjoyed the subject and were a top student but didn't have much interest in teaching it and lacked any clear idea about what you wanted to do in life. Last time he saw you, you were planning to take a year off and get a job in the real world before investing in a master's program. I asked him about extracurricular activities. He thought you were fairly active in some frat house you belonged to before you married, and that you were involved with the Democratic Club on campus. That's as far as I got. I couldn't get ahold of your academic records, which might give an address for your folks, but I'm working on it. The Privacy Act doesn't always make my job easy.''

''I can appreciate that. Is there anything I can do to help speed things up?''

''I could fax your signature with a request for the records to the university. Can you come by my office this afternoon, or tomorrow morning?''

''Just tell me when it's convenient.''

Karen tuned into her own reflections as the two men made plans to meet later. Without asking Ed, she could almost picture the chain of events that had transpired. Because of his early, vague suspicions that Judd wasn't on the up-and-up, he'd probably been concerned when he learned of the mysterious death of Marlene Hall. Her uncle made it a policy to never meddle in police business, so Karen was sure he'd gone to the Creekside Diner and talked to Ricky about Judd solely because he was concerned for his niece's safety. The fact he'd heard everything the waitress had to say and dismissed her suspicions, in light of what he'd learned of Judd's character from his ex and his college advisor, was extremely reassuring.

Karen called up her memories of what she'd learned about abnormal psychology in grad school. Psychopaths were always loners, alienated from others at an early age. Her uncle had probably focused first on Judd's college social life for that reason. And surely, if Judd had ever been angry enough at a woman to want to harm her, it would have been his shrewish and unfaithful first wife.

Uncle Ed finished talking to Judd and turned to her.

"Karen, while I've got you here, I wanted to ask if you know anyone down at the county assessor's office. I got a notice from them yesterday."

As Ed began describing some problem he was having with his property-tax bill, Judd quietly turned his attention to Karen. He was relieved that her shoulders had relaxed from their earlier hunched position, and her hands were limply thrust into the pockets of her coat. Apparently something her uncle had told them had overbalanced whatever fright she contracted at the diner.

"Don't worry," Karen was saying to her uncle. "It's probably just a computer glitch. I'll stop by the assessor's office and get it straightened out."

Judd thanked Ed for everything he'd done and said, "I'll see you at your office today at three."

He lightly touched Karen's elbow to lead her to

the car. He could feel the warmth of her arm right through the coat sleeve, remembered how incredibly soft the skin of her inner arm was. She sent him an affectionate smile as he held the car door open for her, and he imagined he saw a flicker of sexual awareness in the depths of her green eyes, in the slight upturn of her lips. It was like an acknowledgment of a secret connection between them, and very arousing. He had to force his eyes from her shapely legs as she lifted her skirt to get in the car.

Karen couldn't know what fire she was playing with, and he was little wiser than she! What would it take to bring them both to their senses? On the trail above Silver Lake, even in the midst of his anger and her suspicion, there had been an incredible sexual pull between them. It had sent them deep into each other's arms, tapped into a vein of desire so throbbing it had overwhelmed him. He was sure he'd never felt anything even remotely similar with his first wife, nor would again with any woman other than Karen.

Judd jerked his tie loose with one hand as he stepped into the car. He started the engine, and with great effort redirected his thoughts. His next stop should be Marlene Hall's cottage, but he had to finish things with Karen first.

"You know, honey..." The endearment was inappropriate as hell, but it just slipped out. He cleared his throat. "You don't need to fix me any breakfast. I'm really not hungry."

"That's okay." She reached out a hand, tentatively laid it on his shoulder. To his dismay, she inched toward him on the bench seat and leaned her head against his shoulder. It took all his willpower to refrain from reaching his right arm around her shoulders and drawing her even closer.

Devil take it, this was going to be tough! Judd let out a long breath. She sounded tired. Poor woman, she must be exhausted after playing nursemaid to him and his gimpy memory all week. The thought of all she'd had to do for him made him angry.

He owed it to her to explain why he was leaving, to not let her think it was her fault. Then he would pack his things and go.

He tried to think how to begin, what words to say to end it. But the right phrases eluded him, and instead he thought how hungry she must be. He found himself saying, "You should eat something. Why don't we stop and get a sandwich or something? It's almost lunchtime."

"Whatever you like." She sounded a little sleepy, or dreamy.... "I hope I didn't disappoint you, not wanting to go into Granite."

"No, it's better that we stayed here."

They rode in silence for almost a minute, then Karen said, "You're so quiet. Did something my uncle said give you a flashback?"

Her voice was so sweetly hopeful, it made him want to throttle himself. He was a suspected murderer. He didn't deserve her kindness, her concern. She'd be better off feeling sympathy for the snake that had crossed their path. "I'm afraid not."

"Are you mad at me for asking Ed to look into your past, even though you told him not to?"

"No, no, of course not!" His abruptness made her stiffen. "You did the right thing, and I'm in your debt." He added in a more normal tone, "Any new evidence helps at this point." He wanted to say something more, about how she could never possibly do anything to hurt him. That her presence had been the most encouraging, heartening part of this whole nightmarish week. However, he was just minutes from saying goodbye to her for good, and it would be suicidal to reveal any part of his feelings for her now.

At the deli, he insisted she get herself a turkey sandwich and potato salad while he ordered only black coffee for himself. As they returned to the car, he asked, "Is there a park we can go to, somewhere near here, and sit outside while you eat?"

"Sure, there's one by my house." She paused, and her mouth quirked a bit. "It's still pretty cold out. Anyone would think you wanted to enjoy the outdoors before someone locked you up."

Judd's head turned sharply. He recognized it as one of her now familiar attempts to tease him out of a mood, but she must believe profoundly in his innocence to kid him with such a gibe. Well, hard as the truth might be for her, it was time to start making her see it. "Without realizing it," he said, "you read my mind exactly."

Karen blushed, reminding him of a kitten who bats playfully at a moth, only to be surprised and slightly guilty when she catches it. However, she rallied with the rejoinder, "Well, it's about time I learned to read your mind. You're awfully good at doing that to me."

He wanted to do a lot more to her than read her mind, he told himself ruefully. That was part of the problem.

They drove to a small, grassy park near her house. The clouds that had seemed to be lifting earlier were closing in again, threatening to drizzle, and the usual weekend flock of families had abandoned the park. Judd and Karen made for a picnic table under a white wrought-iron gazebo near the kiddies playground.

Karen arranged herself facing the jungle gym, Judd across from her. Her long, water-repellent coat had a flannel lining that promised to keep her warm; however, Judd had on only a single-breasted sport jacket. He didn't seem to notice the chill, though.

As Judd unpacked her lunch for her, she remembered the time, earlier this summer, when she'd walked down here with a neighbor and her two little ones. She'd enjoyed pushing the swing for the five-year-old and playing in the sand with the baby. Now, she pictured Judd beside her in the sand, catching a freckle-faced girl at the bottom of the slide. It was easy to imagine Judd scooping the child up, laughing, pushing the hair out of his eyes as he set her down and took her hand so they could go find Mommy.

Judd cleared his throat, and Karen snapped back to the present. This was no carefree picnic in the park, she reminded herself.

"Would you like half of my sandwich?" she offered.

He didn't say anything, and she had to ask him again before he absently shook his head.

Karen fretted. Despite her earlier attempts to cheer him up with a little kidding, he looked like nothing so much as Socrates contemplating the hemlock. He must be more upset than she'd thought. She dutifully unwrapped her sandwich, but really had no taste for it. She wasn't sure what was bothering him, but she had to make it better before she could bear to swallow even a sip of her soft drink.

She reached for his hand, wrapped her fingers around his hard, work-roughened palm and felt a signal communicate itself like a charge down a line. She gasped, deciphering not a cabled plea for reassurance but a primitive declaration of sexual hunger.

Longing flickered like a smoky candle in the blue gray depths of his eyes. Pent-up desire welled within her, coursed between them on the current of their locked gaze.

Judd was the one to break the connection. He looked down at her hand, lifted it from his own and gently placed it next to her lunch. He cleared his throat, but a telltale huskiness lingered as he said, "You'd better eat."

Karen picked up the sandwich, tried to nibble at it. Though physical intimacy had been only a brief, sporadic part of their relationship, an undercurrent of sexual awareness had existed between them from the beginning. From the first moment they'd met, she'd been acutely aware he was a man, she a woman. Perhaps she should be glad he often seemed to restrain himself from touching her. The force of their attraction was so strong that with one too intimate touch, one too lingering kiss, they might be swept into something neither was ready for.

"We should talk about next steps," Judd said.

"You're right. I'm sorry my uncle upset you." She took a sip of her drink. "I was rather encouraged by what he found."

"I know it sounded good on the surface." Judd laced his fingers. "But you have to consider that I graduated college with a useless diploma, a failed marriage and no direction. If I'd wanted an excuse, I had a perfect one for being frustrated and disgusted with myself. That's probably about the time I took up working in a grease pit, and it sounds like I never had the guts or ambition to rise above it.''

Karen's eyes widened. She'd taken quite a different spin on those facts, but wasn't sure if she should contradict him outright. Much as she didn't agree, there was logic in what he said, and with Judd, that would be hard to counter.

''What happened at the diner?'' he asked. ''Did you overhear something that you haven't told me?''

Karen dug a spoon into her potato salad. She couldn't justify withholding the truth from him any longer, now that she knew revealing it wouldn't place her in any danger from him. And the longer she waited to confess, the more embarrassing and difficult it would be.

She sighed and stirred the salad so she wouldn't have to meet his eyes.

''You're right.'' Shucks, she was always telling him he was right. How inept he must find her. ''I wasn't completely forthcoming about that. In fact, I *was* able to talk for a while with one of the waitresses. The older one, Ricky Black is her name. Apparently Uncle Ed interviewed her last night, too, and he seemed to think she was mostly full of hot air, but you have the right to know what she's telling everyone.''

Karen looked up, afraid he was going to ask her why she hadn't told him this when she left the diner, but he simply waited, sober faced, for her to go on.

She told him what Ricky had said about Judd's friendship with Marlene, about Marlene's personality and her need for privacy that kept her from sharing the details of her love life with her co-workers, and about Marlene calling Ricky the night she was killed to say she was going out of town. Karen finished by repeating a point she'd already made twice. "No one has any evidence that you were the man Marlene was seeing. There isn't even any proof she was planning to go away *with* someone. It's all assumption."

Judd made no attempt to respond as he listened to Karen argue for his innocence. The horror of what he might have done to Marlene clawed at him from one side, while Karen's selfless concern and utter sincerity pulled from the other. It was like being torn physically in two.

He tried to drag his eyes from hers and couldn't. How could he ever leave this tender, desirable woman, who had come to mean everything to him, and not cease to care about living? They might as well pronounce the death sentence on him now. She was so agonizingly beautiful, with all that trembling anxiety in her voice. Even when she was trying to be logical and professional, her eyes were vulnerable, pleading with him to agree with her.

He buried his head in his hands. He was all twisted up inside, sick at heart from loving her and fearing what he might be capable of doing to her. He couldn't trust himself to remain near her one more hour. He would hurt her one way or the other, emotionally—or, please God no, physically—whether he wanted to or not. He savagely scrubbed his face with the heels of his palms, then stared past her at nothing, dreading what he had to say.

Karen waited, alarmed at how tormented he appeared. Had he been sleeping at all? He didn't look it. Eerily, at that moment he said, "I have to be honest with you, too, Karen. I've been having some terrible nightmares. They started in the hospital, and continued at my apartment. I thought they were gone, until this morning when I had another. In these dreams, I see the faces of several young women. They are dead, their throats cut, and looking at them I feel this incredible sense of anger. Of murderous rage.

"At first I couldn't see the faces clearly, or at least couldn't remember them when I awoke, I'm not sure which. But this morning, when I unfolded the newspaper and saw the photo of Marlene on the front page, I realized she was one of the faces in my dream."

An icy coldness enveloped Karen. But this time, she knew in her soul there must be another explanation for what he'd experienced. She would never again doubt him, as she had so easily before.

While Judd shifted in his seat to stare bleakly at the deserted playground, she quickly compared what he'd said to what she'd learned about human psychology both on the job and in her many years of training to be a social worker.

"Judd."

He reluctantly faced her.

"Dreams are strange things, and we know that memories from your past can surface at any time. Because you were acquainted with Marlene, and probably liked her since she was a nice girl, and because you've been so troubled that she was killed, it makes sense that your subconscious mind would bring up her picture while you slept and insert it in your nightmare.

"Have you considered, too," she continued, "that you might have witnessed Marlene's murder? Perhaps you *were* close friends and had made arrangements to take a trip together. When you arrived at her house to pick her up, you could have found her body, or even walked in as she was being killed. That would also explain the anger you feel—you could be mad at the killer, not the women victims."

Judd shook his head impatiently. "I've thought of that, but it doesn't add up. If I'd found Marlene dead, why didn't I pick up her phone and immediately call the police? If I interrupted the murder, surely the killer would have tried to take me out, too, but there were no signs I'd been in a fight. Or if I witnessed the murder unobserved and fled, why did they find me in my car, headed out of town? Wouldn't I have stopped at the first house down the road and asked to use their phone to call the police?"

"I don't know, but I'm sure there's a reasonable explanation. Together we can piece together what really happened."

Judd's broad shoulders hunched in frozen misery. Icy glints of rage gathered in the depths of his eyes. He shook his head slowly. "No, we can't do it together, Karen. You can only make it worse. I have to get away from here, away from you."

A SHINY WHITE sedan and two Silver Creek police units idled in front of Karen's house as Judd and Karen pulled up. Lieutenant Rossini, his partner, Talmadge, and a pair of uniformed cops rushed forward as Judd exited his car.

"Mr. Maxwell, would you place your hands on the top of the vehicle," the lead detective ordered.

Judd slowly reached for the hood, and Talmadge began frisking him. The hands of the edgy patrolmen hovered over their holstered guns.

"We're taking you in for questioning regarding the murder of Marlene Hall," Rossini said. "Talmadge, read him his rights while I show Ms. Thomas the warrant to search her house."

Chapter Twelve

It was almost 8:00 p.m. when they let him go. Judd picked his jacket off the back of the chair and slung it over his shoulder as he preceded Lieutenant Rossini from the interrogation room. The offices opening off the dimly lit hallway were deserted on this Saturday evening, the two men silent with fatigue and mutual distrust.

Not counting the time it took for fingerprinting, Judd estimated he had been in that room almost six hours. He noted his mind was a little fuzzy now, his back and legs tired, but that was merely from sitting all day. He could probably go another twenty, twenty-four before he needed sleep, and then just a couple of hours.

Judd's brain switched from the assessment of his endurance to examine the strange, almost absolute detachment he'd assumed. All through the afternoon and evening, as the detectives had interrogated him, called breaks, then returned to repeat the same questions, he had been curiously outside himself. Like an invisible counselor, he had advised the subject Judd how to respond, watched Judd speak and evaluated the cops' reactions.

It had been helpful. He'd been able to set aside any foreboding he might have felt sitting across from the law, undoubtedly being studied by a prosecutor and a curious honcho or two from the other side of the one-way glass set in the wall. He had endured the tedium of being asked, over and over again, questions he could not answer. And he'd kept cool when a frustrated Rossini baited him, and later told him outright that he was a lying scum.

Judd scowled as Rossini punched the elevator button to take them to the first floor. Beneficial as the objectivity was, it was also distinctly ominous. How had Rossini put it? "Maxwell, you're the coolest damn murderer I've ever met."

The car arrived with a ping, and Rossini followed him in. Had this emotional disassociation helped him kill his victims? Was the amnesia just one further step in a pathological separation process that had enabled him to commit unspeakable crimes? Perhaps he'd been killing and temporarily forgetting for years, only this time the memory loss had lasted for more than a few hours and drawn him to the attention of the authorities. When he began to regain his memory, would he recall other murders, or had he blocked those out forever? For a moment, he considered which would be worse. To live with the full, horrible knowledge of one's crimes, and accept one's execution as just punishment. Or to face the death chamber unsure if one deserved it or was innocent, to die having recalled nothing more than garbled, unreliable dreams.

The elevator arrived in the reception area of the sheriff's office. Without a word, Judd stepped out, and Rossini hit a button to return upstairs. They had

said everything they had to say to one another for
now. Judd had no doubt they'd be seeing each other
again soon enough.

The uniformed clerk at the counter spoke to Judd.
"Mr. Maxwell? There's someone waiting for you in
the cafeteria." The young man gestured through the
glass double doors that led to the rest of the hall of
justice. "Down the main corridor, on the left."

Judd silently pushed through the cafeteria door.
She was sitting at a round table, her back turned
three-quarters from him, staring dully at the coffee
machines, a paper cup curled in her right hand. She
was clearly exhausted, her dress wrinkled, as though
she'd slept in it.

He wondered with annoyance how Karen could be
so lovely when she was so disheveled. No makeup,
not even lipstick. Her hair was tousled and needed a
good brushing. But he was as drawn to her now as
he would have been were she dressed in silk and
coiffed like a movie star.

He could feel his pulse quicken. He wanted to
bend over her from behind, push aside her russet hair
and taste the soft, sensitive spot he'd found beneath
her ear. He wanted to lift her to her feet and press
her hips against the table, run his hands around her
rib cage. He wanted to unbutton the front of her dress
and kiss her ripe, warm breasts, forget who he was
and where they were.

It was getting difficult to breathe. "Karen?" he
said as he bent toward her.

Karen started and her head whipped around. He
loomed just inches above her, fully aware that the
lights above them would make a dark silhouette of

his torso. He let his expression go icy as he stared at her.

"If you want to stay alive," he hissed, "you'll get the hell out of here."

Karen turned back to the table and cleared her throat. "I, ah, brought your car. You left the key in the ignition. Would you like a cup of coffee before we go?" Her hand shook as she pulled her purse toward her and began searching for some change.

"What I want is for you to disappear."

Judd ground his teeth. Karen wasn't only beautiful and bighearted, but she was too damn smart, as well. Instead of trailing him to Granite City in her own car, which would have been the natural thing to do, she'd driven his. She knew he would have hitched a ride back to Silver Creek to get his car, but that he wouldn't leave her here to do the same. Like it or not, he was stuck driving her home.

"Are you hungry? I can't believe they kept you in there this long."

Fatigue got the best of him. He decided to delay sparring with her temporarily, and sat down as he spoke. "Without arresting me, you mean? They were mad as could be at having to let me go, but apparently the D.A. needs just one more shred of evidence before they can legally hold me."

"I know."

Judd was mesmerized by the swing of her hips as Karen maneuvered out of her seat and stepped to the coffee machine. "Lieutenant Rossini found out I was here and came out to talk to me, about an hour ago. He tried to convince me to have nothing further to do with you." Her gaze briefly, defiantly, met his as she handed him the cup of black coffee. "I told him to mind his own business."

He wanted like anything to grin, but he didn't allow the signal of approval to reach his face. Just being in the same room with her was too comforting by half; before he knew it, she'd gotten him feeling more relaxed, letting his guard down, tempting him to converse with her normally. He finished the coffee in one last, scalding swallow, crumpled the cup in his hand and hammered it like a fastball into a trash can across the room. The hour's ride to Silver Creek, sitting inches from her in the front seat, was going to be like a trip to hell.

KAREN WAS TRYING to convince him he was no psychopath as Judd swung the Chevy onto Highway 18. Apparently she'd taken a course in abnormal psychology and had watched a few documentaries on serial killers. So now she was an expert!

"Damn it, Karen." He was finished restraining himself. It was time to make her wake up. "I know I didn't fit the profile of a psychopath in college, according to the little your uncle was able to dig up. But don't you see, by the time I graduated my life was going downhill, and who knows what I've been through in the ten years since then! This amnesia could be only a temporary reprieve from inner demons you can't even imagine.

"Remember when I told you I have a strong distrust of other people, that I somehow felt I hadn't always been this way? That paranoia could be just a hint of the latent, hostile, antisocial feelings that have grown up over the years. In plain English, I could be very sick."

Karen started to protest, but he cut her off with a hatchetlike motion. "Is it worth risking your life that I'm not a Dr. Jekyll and Mr. Hyde? That I won't turn on you when my memories surface? It's what the police are scared to death of. Rossini warned me he'd personally hunt me down and put a bullet through me if I lay a finger on you."

Karen eyed him with grave concern, unable to form a response. His voice, let alone the words, were so bitter, his countenance contorted with loathing for himself. Yet, tortured as he was, his first concern was not for himself, but for her.

She had never felt more drawn to him than she did at this moment. It was terrible to see him demoralized like this, yet there was something honorable and magnificent in his self-condemnation. Had he reacted more calmly to the horrific accusations of the police, or begun to make even the smallest excuse to justify his alleged acts, she would have instantly lost all love for him. Instead, she felt a tremendous respect for Judd Maxwell the man, and a new certainty in his innocence.

"I'm a drifter, Karen, a bum who can't even keep a full-time job." The ragged breath he took seemed to fuel the fire in his eyes. "I never told you this, but the day I got my car back, the Department of Motor Vehicles let me know I have driver's licenses in California, Nevada, Oregon and Washington. What kind of person lives in four states in ten years? I'll tell you—someone on the run. The detectives asked me a hell of a lot of questions about those other residences. I wouldn't be surprised if they're linking me to a series of similar killings in little towns all over the west."

Karen set her lips in a line and folded her arms tightly.

''And that day at your uncle's, when he had me fire his gun—you didn't realize I was faking it, but I *knew* how to use that piece. I could have nailed the target blindfolded, but I wanted to keep it a secret from you.''

Karen closed her eyes, trying to shut out Judd's unbearable pain, but the picture of his tortured face remained in her mind. She considered telling him she knew about his familiarity with firearms, that her uncle had suspected him of deliberately missing the target, and that despite that, Ed believed him innocent. But she doubted that would reassure Judd.

For the second time that day, tears threatened to well up. She wanted desperately to say something that would ease his self-doubts, anything that would encourage him to believe in himself the way she believed in him. But she sensed intuitively that if she argued with him any longer, he might explode. She'd be a fool to push him any further.

HE'D GIVEN HER more than enough to frighten her. Enough hard, chilling facts to fuel her nightmares for months to come. As they rode silently the rest of the way to Karen's house, Judd became sure he'd reached his objective and scared her out of his life forever.

He couldn't avoid the thought that these were perhaps the last minutes they would spend together. He clamped down on the maudlin reflection. He couldn't afford weakness in any form, whether it be sentimentality, or true love, or regret.

He tested her as they pulled up to her house; she

wouldn't meet his gaze, looked anxiously away. The tension was thick as she walked ahead of him to the front door and let them in. He watched her scramble for the electric switch to avoid being caught in the dark with him.

"You'd better go to your room, Karen," he told her back, "and lock the door." He thought he saw her shoulders shiver, could feel her fear as she almost ran to the back of•the house.

He stood immobile in the living room, his chest so tight he had to fight to inhale. Impatiently he shoved a hand through his hair, pushing back the darkness that fell over his sight as he stared at the hallway she'd fled down. He thought this afternoon that he'd conquered his feelings for her.

Close up the wound, Maxwell, he told himself, you're bleeding all over the place! She's just a woman. You can still manage to walk, and eat, and drink and talk without her. They don't require much of you where you're going—to prison. You can still maintain the forms of living.

If you ever find another reason to.

Slowly the familiar, blessed numbness returned to him. Mechanically he grabbed his already packed suitcase. The sheriff's boys had made a mess of things when they searched his possessions. He stuffed a shirtsleeve back in so he could close the zipper. His pet cockatiel, awakened by his return, whistled imploringly from its cage. Judd barely heard.

He tried vaguely to remember if he'd packed his shaving kit in the suitcase. He didn't really care about it, but he didn't want to leave any of his belongings behind for Karen to deal with. He glanced down as he set the case on the floor, and heard Karen quietly padding into the room.

What could she possibly want with him now? Was she about to deliver some incredibly misplaced apology for not being able to help him?

He looked up to find her standing, uncertainly, perhaps ten feet from him. The lovely sight of her transfixed him. She'd changed into a pink cotton nightgown and matching robe. The robe was open in the front, the tie string hanging free. The matching fulllength gown hung straight below the swell of her breasts, demurely hiding her legs, but the neckline was low, exposing even more of her creamy flesh through a cutwork motif.

He was flushed with an almost uncontrollable desire to push the wrap back off her shoulders, to press his hands through the thin cloth and fondle her breasts. Already he was growing stiff for her, a pulse throbbing against his fly. Devil take him, his brutish reaction was purely unintentional on her part, he was sure. She couldn't possibly know how sexy she was.

"Judd," she said with a tremulous smile. She was like a shy puppy, waiting for a sign of friendship to approach him.

She was so achingly sweet, so innocent. Her femininity called up every instinct within him to protect her. He gritted his teeth. He *would* protect her, from everything and everyone— especially from himself.

"Karen, go back to your room, *now*."

But instead of obeying him, she took a tentative step forward. Her smooth, maidenly fingers came up to the opening in her robe, began to delicately draw the fabric down her arms.

"No!" He grasped her hands in his own rough

paws, crushing her fragile bones as he attempted to stop her, but when he released her hands, the robe slipped from her arms to the floor.

He was horrified. What did she think she was doing? Offering herself? Like a sacrificial virgin to a heathen god? She couldn't possibly know how incredibly aroused he was. Or if she did, why didn't she fear that he might take her by force? Didn't she realize that the release of his sexual energy might be the very catalyst to unleash the hidden demons within him? That the act of loving her could trigger a sick desire to kill her? Couldn't she sense that making love with him would be wildly dangerous?

He wanted her so badly now, it was like a destructive force, an impulse to ravage her so strong it felt like madness. He swung away from her, fists flexing at his sides, nails digging into his palms. Unreasoning rage grew within him, flowed like molten lava into his limbs. As in his nightmares, he could feel only the anger that consumed him so completely— though he couldn't fathom where it came from, couldn't try to understand it. He only knew what he must do. He must hurt her, physically.

Karen waited tensely as she watched Judd's stooped back, his taut shoulders. A strange mixture of attraction and fear tickled at her as she tried to reassure herself. She guessed he was feeling unworthy of her, struggling with his highly developed conscience. At least, that was what she hoped.... He'd never seemed quite so formidable as he did now, his tremendous strength evident in the bulging back muscles beneath the stressed fabric of his jacket.

He inhaled sharply, and she thought she heard his breath tremble as he released it. Thank goodness, he was coming around, softening toward her, and himself! But when he spun to face her, she knew she was wrong. There was no vulnerability in his countenance, only murderous rage.

He hurtled toward her, right arm raised above his head at a ghastly angle, teeth bared like a wolf's. With a cry, she turned her face away and squeezed her eyes shut, bracing for the blow.

She felt the heat of his chest halt inches from her face, the heaving respiration above her ear, but he didn't touch her.

"Come on," she quavered, then the strength of her own pent-up tension charged her voice. "Hit me, Judd. Do it now, damn you. If you can do it, show me!"

But nothing happened.

Cautiously Karen opened her eyes.

Judd gradually lowered his arm like a broken javelin. Sweat covered his forehead and inched toward his beard. Deep lines scarred his cheeks, and tears of bewilderment moistened his eyelashes. He looked like a man who had just failed to save a child from the wheels of a speeding truck.

"You see," she said, tears in her voice, "you couldn't do it, could you?"

He stared without comprehension at her.

"You couldn't do it, could you, Judd?" She reached up and cupped his bearded jaw in her palm. "Tell me the truth. Not all the demons in hell could make you hurt me."

"No," he said bitterly, "they couldn't."

Joy suffused her being. "Don't you see! I knew you wouldn't harm me. I knew you couldn't." She fell into his arms.

"But Karen—"

"I had to show you, darling. That's why I told you to hit me, to make you see you're not a monster."

The import of her words registered somewhere within his mind, but on the surface, Judd wasn't listening. The dusty, rose-petal smell of her hair was intoxicating to him. The pressure of her soft, voluptuous body against his pushed aside all thought but the desire to utterly consume her, to taste and touch and command every part of her.

Her earnest expression sought his. "I believe in you, Judd, darling. No matter what, I'm going to stand by you."

Her words finally broke through then, their warmth finding a way to his soul. As the revelation struck him, he comprehended what she'd done, what she'd succeeded in proving to him.

With a mighty roar, the dam of reserve broke in his heart and all his love and passion for her burst forth. Like a man reprieved from a death sentence, he hungrily, joyously kissed her mouth, her cheeks, her eyelids. All he knew was, she was pliant in his arms, yielding as he ran his hands over her exquisite back and down to her bottom, marveling at her soft curves, trailing kisses to the sweet flesh at the line of her nightdress.

The impulse to rip the gown off stopped him. With great effort, he banked his desire enough to pull back and search her.

"I love you, Karen," he said solemnly, "and I want to make love to you."

"I feel the same way, Judd." There was a modest tremor in her voice, but he couldn't mistake the dusky film of desire in her eyes. It excited and enchanted him. On impulse he bent and swept her off her feet. She felt light as a fairy queen as she clung to him, her silken head nesting below his chin. Glory, he wanted to shout! She made him feel strong as ten men.

He kicked aside the robe, strode to her bedroom and across to her bed, then hesitated over the white eyelet comforter with her delicious weight in his arms. She was inexperienced, and he mustn't rush her. It didn't feel humanly possible to stop now, but he would. He pivoted from the bed, set her down carefully on her feet.

Her emerald eyes shone trustingly up at him as a smile trembled on her lips. She seemed to be willing him to take her, to teach her what love was. It was an awesome responsibility.... He must be gentle as a man could be, mustn't frighten her or bruise her fragile feminine loveliness. She was so precious to him— he was almost afraid to begin, and unsure how. His hands came up reflexively to touch her hair. He buried his fingers in the rich umber, arranged the tresses over her shoulders and watched with fascination how the crushed curls sprang back when he released them.

Karen closed her eyes, her mind finally at peace as Judd stroked her hair. It was blissful to be released from all worries about his former life. The details of his past no longer mattered to her, couldn't matter, because she'd seen the essence of his character. He was every inch the man she'd waited so long for, and now knew she loved—principled, self-sacrificing, brave and coolheaded in the face of danger. A man who had proved he could weather the deepest trials by bending but never breaking or compromising his honor. Someone she could willingly love, honor and cherish for the rest of her life.

Judd caressed her neck with his lips. As he nibbled gently at the tender skin, she groaned, the sigh soft and raspy, full of all the yearning she felt for him.

Judd made an answering growl deep in his throat. "Oh, Karen, you make my head swim." His exploring mouth moved to her collarbone, and the proximity of his lips awoke a tingling in her ribs. She could feel her breasts swell, reminding her intensely that she was a female, fashioned to complement his maleness in every respect, and soon he would show her the deepest meaning of what it was to be a woman.

She willed him to go on, gripping his shoulders and arching into him, feeling her nipples rub his fully clothed chest through the gauzy nightgown. The sensation was wanton, and at the same time primally fulfilling. In response, Judd reached down, bunched a handful of her gown and lifted the hem. She raised her arms, wiggling a bit to help him as he slipped the garment over her head.

Judd inhaled sharply. It sounded like a compliment, but she was unsure. Feeling cherished and abandoned had been easy fully clothed, but nude, her self-consciousness about her body returned, and she remembered how she had always been too big-boned, too ample to be attractive.

"Karen, you're lovely," Judd whispered.

She opened her eyes. Pearly moonlight filtered over them through the sheer curtains, and Judd was drinking her in with appreciative eyes.

Lovingly he took hold of her hands. "You *are* beautiful," he breathed, "like a painting." He shook his head in gentle wonder. "One of the old masters might have conceived you as the perfect woman."

With newborn trust, and from a desire to please him, she timidly squeezed his fingers. He returned the pressure, his steady, admiring gaze as much a balm to her femininity as his physical caresses had been.

"This is selfish of me," he said finally, "I could look at you all night, but you must be cold. Get under the covers, and I'll join you in a minute."

Karen obeyed, lying quietly against the pillows as Judd undressed. As he removed each garment, he threw it over the back of her tapestry-covered slipper chair. The last to go were his briefs, then he paused, perhaps allowing her a turn to look at him.

It was the first time she'd seen a completely naked man. She didn't want to stare, but he really was magnificent. He himself would have made a model for an artist—a Greek sculpting the long-ago champion of the first Olympic Games. Though her gaze skimmed it only briefly, it was impossible to overlook his considerable arousal.

As he drew back the covers and slid in beside her, he smiled, white teeth flashing in the moonlight. He nuzzled her forehead playfully with his beard, and she reached up.

"It *is* soft," Karen said, stroking his jaw with her fingertips, then trying her cheek against it. "I can't tell you how many times I've wanted to touch your face."

Unable to resist her curiosity, she let her fingers move downward to the firm, warm flesh of his chest. Fascinated, she probed her hand below the sheet to his stomach. Through his slightly coarse dusting of hair, she squeezed his upper abdominals; they were dense with muscle.

"If you go much farther, sweetheart, it will be a short evening," he said.

"I'm sorry." She jerked her hand back, but he caught it and kissed it. "Don't be embarrassed, I was only teasing. I love it when you touch me."

He started to reach for her, then unexpectedly rolled onto his back and put his forearm over his eyes.

"What's wrong?" she asked.

He muffled a curse. "I can't believe I forgot about this until now, but—" he uncovered his eyes to look at her "—we really shouldn't be doing this without..." His voice trailed off in regret.

Karen's eyes widened as she caught his meaning. "You're right. But..." She fished in her nightstand and pressed a few gold foil coins into his hand. "One of my associates works with young, unmarried mothers," she explained, "and she insisted on giving me these."

He regarded her solemnly. "I guessed this was your first time. It is, isn't it?"

Uneasily she replied, "Does it matter?"

"Yes, because it makes this incredibly special." He rolled toward her and propped himself on his elbow. "And, I have to confess, it makes me both very glad...and rather nervous."

"You've done this before," she said, feeling both more at ease because of it, and a little jealous of the other women he'd known.

"I can't remember another time," he said, his hand cradling her cheek. "To tell you the truth, sweetheart, I hope I never do."

Karen kissed his palm, then held his gaze for a pregnant second before closing her lids as a signal for him to begin.

He didn't hurry, embroidering her collarbone with little kisses. He eased the sheet back, began lightly circling her breasts with the pads of his thumbs, then slowly deepening the pressure into a delectable massage, sending tendrils of erotic sensation downward to her abdomen. To reciprocate, Karen kneaded the dense tissue of his shoulders. His neck was as corded as an oak, but the shaved hair at the back of his head felt like velvet when she stroked it.

Judd's heated mouth came down, and he licked the contour of her right breast, each heady stroke of his tongue filling her with fire. When he took the nipple between his lips and gently worried it, the pleasure grew indescribable.

His long fingers circled her waist, the thumbs splaying over her tummy, exacerbating a ravishing hunger deep in her womanly parts.

"Judd, darling." She whispered the words like a prayer. Then, as he raised his head, she urged, "Don't stop, please."

"I won't, I promise."

He continued to pleasure her breast with his tongue as his broad hands smoothed languorously over her belly, trailing promise and fire over her pubic mound, then reached wickedly between her legs.

Karen gasped, her hands fisting in the bedsheet.

"Karen, you're breathtaking," Judd said, his fingers searching her moist folds. "If I'm not careful, you'll drive me wild."

"Fair is fair," she managed to gasp.

The bed rocked like a boat as he positioned himself; Karen's heart beat an erratic tattoo.

He lowered his heavy body over her, blocking out the moonlight, and braced himself on one elbow as his other hand continued to stroke her with incredible tenderness. "This may be a little uncomfortable at first," he whispered.

She didn't care; she felt ready to burst.

A moment that divided time later, he asked anxiously, "Am I hurting you?"

She wanted to laugh, she loved him so much. "No, for a second perhaps, but not now. Quite the contrary, darling." She wrapped her arms about him, holding him close as she soaked in the wondrously satisfying sensation of being one with him. An involuntary spasm rolled through her.

The movement seemed to excite him, and the intense feelings were soon doubled by the ravishing friction Judd created inside her. He moved rhythmically, consistently, rocking like the waves of the ocean. Karen could feel an erotic pressure begin to build and build within her.

As a rapturous storm swelled between them, she wrapped her arms around Judd's sweating back, her breathing marking time with his fervid thrusts.

Karen clung desperately to her lover, the pilot of her soul, trusting him to bring them home through the turbulent sea of passion. When the ecstatic pressure grew too much to bear, she called out his name, and with a flurry of masterful strokes he brought them both in, exhausted but safe, beached on the shores of Paradise.

They lay entwined, lungs heaving, minds insensible to all emotions but joy. Momentarily drained of strength, Judd used the last ounce he had to draw Karen tightly to his chest. Her arms still encircled him like a golden band, and he found himself saying a heartfelt prayer of thanks for her.

His lady had given him indescribable gifts tonight, first helping him to see himself through her eyes, not as a man deranged but as someone worthy of a good woman's faith. And now, she had made herself completely vulnerable to him, given him the greatest, most precious gift of love and trust that a woman could bestow.

Judd buried his face in his precious love's hair and drew a deep breath of her unique scent. Karen Thomas was everything wise and womanly and wonderful in this world. Even as he had released himself into her, he had felt her miraculous essence flowing into him—saving him, healing him, renewing him. He still did not know who he had been in the past, but Judd was very sure that this night had changed who he would be forever.

THEY SLEPT IN the next morning. Judd awoke close to nine, rolled over instinctively in search of Karen's soft form and teetered at the edge of the sofa.

Where was he? He pushed the hair from his forehead, afraid for a disoriented second. Had it all been a dream? Had last night been only a thrilling flight of his imagination? He was on Karen's couch. No, he must have sleepwalked again. Last night had been real, thank God. The most real night of his life!

He walked naked to the kitchen and started a pot of coffee, the total awareness that he was in love with Karen Thomas, and she, with him, zinging in his veins. The sky outside the kitchen window was overcast, but the memory of their intense lovemaking warmed his blood, for he felt no chill.

On the way to the shower, he checked on her. His heart stirred as he watched Karen from the bedroom doorway, her cheek buried in the pillow, her fox-colored hair fanning over one round, delicious shoulder. The sheet, unfortunately, was pinned primly between her arm and body. He had an impulse to enter the room and awake her in the sweetest way possible. But compassion bade him let her sleep; she was probably exhausted after staying up so late, and there would be time for love after breakfast.

It wasn't until he was midway through a hot shower that the full memory of yesterday's arrest and interrogation suddenly returned to Judd. As the weight of his trouble settled on him again, he could only wonder that being with Karen had so completely pushed it from his mind. From the minute he picked her up to carry her to the bedroom, his every sense, every thought—even every dream as he slept—had been filled with her. Though in a way it troubled him that he'd temporarily put aside such a pressing matter, on the other hand, he was glad the tragedy of Marlene hadn't interfered with his lovemaking with Karen.

As he dressed in jeans and a polo shirt, Judd decided to delay thinking about the case just a little bit longer. Right after breakfast, he must go to Marlene's house—the newspapers described it as a cottage in the woods—and take a look at the crime scene. If it wasn't too early, he'd stop at Ed Thomas's office on the way and sign that release letter for his college records.

He realized it might be foolish to delay his investigation, but for now, he wanted just one more hour, to fix breakfast for himself and Karen, to wake her and eat with her, before returning to the chaos that was the rest of his life.

He turned the little radio on in the kitchen while he cooked. The classical-music station was too heavy for the buoyant mood he wanted to sustain, so he dialed through the channels. An agitated male voice piqued his curiosity and made him listen:

"…don't have a good feeling about this at all, folks, I'm sorry to say. In fact, I was alone in the studio this morning, I'd just started the broadcast at five, when I heard a kind of pop. This booth is basically soundproof, and I thought at the time it must be an awfully loud backfire from a car. That was approximately four hours ago. Our engineer has gone downstairs where the police cars and unmarked vehicles have gathered and he should be reporting back in just—here he is!

"Rusty, can you tell us what is going on outside the radio station here in downtown Silver Creek?"

"Yes. Apparently it's worse than we feared, Mike. One of the suites in our small office complex here is rented by a gentleman, an older man who works as a private investigator. Apparently he has been shot to death."

Chapter Thirteen

"Rusty," the announcer said, "we have to break for a quick commercial. We'll be right back, folks."

Judd stared at the radio in shock. When Ed Thomas had given him directions to his office the day before, he had mentioned the tiny radio station upstairs. There could be no mistake— Karen's uncle was dead. She would be crushed. She had never talked much about her relationship with Thomas, but it had been clear to Judd that her affection for him ran deep....

The man had been murdered. It had to be—the PI had shown no signs of being suicidal when they spoke with him. It was too much of a coincidence.

A jolt went through Judd as he made the connection: he'd been sleepwalking last night, awaking in the living room.... But *surely* he couldn't have left the house and murdered a man in his sleep! Even if he'd been in a trance, some crazy altered state, he would have to be utterly mad to carry off a killing and not remember it. Besides that, he didn't have a gun.

Judd dismissed the notion of his own guilt. Yesterday, perhaps, he would have entertained the possibility, taken more time to consider it, but he was less ready to believe himself a murderer today, after Karen had proved so completely what utter faith she had in him.

However, the police would have no trouble believing he was responsible! Thomas had been talking to the crew at the Creekside Diner about the murder, probably asking questions about his niece's suspicious client all over town. A desire to silence the investigator, who might have learned too much, would be motive enough for the police. They were probably on their way to arrest him now.

Judd pictured himself being led away in handcuffs, a judge setting bail, and a tearful Karen struggling to post a bond for him. Or worse, since this was a conservative, rural community, his bail request might be denied entirely. He might be trapped in jail and never get a chance to look into his own past and his connection with Marlene Hall, and meanwhile, the detectives would stop looking for the real killer, convinced they had the perpetrator behind bars. No, he couldn't let them take him in, not until he had answers to some of his own questions.

He started to the bedroom to wake Karen, then stopped, his mind racing. It would take several minutes to rouse her, and she was sure to be grief-stricken and in shock when she heard about her uncle. There wasn't time to break the news gently *and* explain his plans. Judd chewed savagely on his lip. He hated like hell to leave Karen this way, but an explanatory note would have to suffice.

As he grabbed a pencil beside the kitchen phone, his hypersensitive ears picked up the sound of automobiles approaching on the street. There were three, maybe more, large engines.

He threw down the pencil. The house would be completely surrounded in a matter of seconds. He'd scoped out Karen's backyard his first day here. There was a vine-covered gate at the back that led to a dirt lane behind the house.

He paused at the sunporch door just long enough to scan the landscape, then sprinted to the fence. As he ran, he could hear car doors slamming out front. The gate was stuck fast at its foot by years of accumulated leaf debris. He stepped back, took two running steps and vaulted. As he cleared the top, a voice behind shouted, "There he is—going over the back fence. Get him!"

KAREN WAS AWAKENED by the simultaneous sounds of the bell ringing and someone thumping on the front door. She'd been deep asleep and peered hazily at the clock: 9:40. Where was Judd, and why wasn't he answering the door? Perhaps he'd gone jogging. It wouldn't surprise her. That man had energy to burn, that was for sure. She gave a satisfied grin.

But her amusement turned to alarm as the pounding continued and shouts came from her backyard. She threw aside the covers and peeked out the curtained window. Men, in uniform she thought, were milling around at the back of the yard. The intervening shrubbery made it impossible to tell what they were doing, but the sight of them turned her blood to ice.

She shoved her most concealing terry-cloth robe over her nightdress, gave up on finding her slippers and hurried to the door barefoot.

"Ms. Thomas, would you step aside please, ma'am."

Detective Talmadge and a cop in blue swept past her. They were here for Judd. Her head swam. Through the sunporch, she watched more police run across the yard. Lieutenant Rossini appeared in their wake, barking orders.

Something told her Judd wasn't here; she hadn't seen him on her way to the door, and the house felt empty. She drifted into the living room and stood by the cockatiel's cage. Judd had forgotten to cover it last night, and Trouble was clinging to his perch, his body slim and rigid with fright at the sudden invasion of these agitated strangers.

The cops made a thorough search of the house. Just as they finished and regrouped in the living room, Lieutenant Rossini came in. Talmadge raised his brows; his partner just barely shook his head and said nothing.

"You men," Rossini addressed the uniformed officers, "join the sergeant outside."

Karen found her tongue. "I take it you've gotten your warrant for Judd's arrest." She knew there was no point in being testy, but she couldn't keep the caustic combination of anger and fear from her voice.

The senior detective searched her face for a moment, then gestured toward the sofa. "Deputy Talmadge and I need to talk to you, if you don't mind."

The lieutenant's voice had softened incredibly to a tone she'd never heard; an instinctive reaction made her stomach turn over. She wrapped the robe tightly about her legs and sat down. The partners took seats across from her.

"I have some bad news for you, Ms. Thomas,"

Rossini began. He started to remove a notebook from his breast pocket, then stopped and forced his eyes back to Karen. "I'm sorry to have to break it to you like this, but your uncle, Edward Thomas, was found dead in his office this morning."

Karen's heart stopped. She'd heard him correctly, as clear as day, but was he lying? Was this some tactic to get her to tell them where Judd was? She searched their faces: Rossini's mouth drooped in a grimace, and his fist was clenched so tight the knuckles were white; young Talmadge stared at the carpet as he sniffed and ran a finger under his nose. Altogether their body language seemed genuine and unrehearsed.

"Ms. Thomas," Rossini said quietly, "your uncle was murdered." He continued over Karen's cry, "We are as sure as we can be that Judd Maxwell shot him, and we need your help to find Maxwell and bring him to justice."

"Oh, my God. Oh, my God." Karen buried her face in her hands. Her thoughts flew in all directions. She tried to hang on to rationality, to marshal the questions that would prove this all a terrible mistake. "Are you sure it's my uncle? When did it happen? It couldn't have been Judd—he was with me all night, right here."

Talmadge shot his partner a look that seemed to say *The bastard*. He cleared his throat. "Another tenant of the building heard a shot just after five this morning. Mr. Thomas's body was discovered in his office an hour ago. Think back, Ms. Thomas, are you sure Maxwell was here *all* night? Could you have been asleep and he slipped away?"

Karen swallowed the tears that formed in her

throat. She'd dozed off around two, with Judd beside her. She'd slept like a baby the remainder of the night, never waking even to use the bathroom.

"Yes," she admitted, "it's possible. But that doesn't mean it happened."

"Do you know where Maxwell is?"

"No. I was asleep when you arrived." They regarded her skeptically, and she was forced to add, "I, ah, didn't see Judd this morning."

Rossini took up the questioning again. "Do you have any idea where he might go if he's on the run?"

Things were moving much too fast for her. This whole thing was impossible. Unreal. She still wasn't sure she could trust these two. She held up her palms to silence them. "Please, could we slow down? You say someone shot my uncle." How strange and horrible the words sounded. She had to steel herself to speak them. "But are you sure? He cleans his guns a lot, they're his hobby. Are you…are you sure he wasn't just—?"

Rossini shook his head. "This was no accident, Ms. Thomas. There would have been powder burns on the body if he'd been holding the gun up close. Maxwell fired from across the room. They were clean, well-aimed shots to the head."

"Oh, no!" Karen clutched her stomach and bent double. She looked up to find Talmadge, beside her, holding a glass of water. She teetered on the edge of hysteria for long minutes, then began to pull herself back. When she dimly realized she'd made a mess of the sleeve of her robe, she got up and retrieved a box of tissues from the nightstand in her room. The sight of the rumpled sheets on the bed made her feel as though her whole insides were caving in.

"Ms. Thomas," Rossini said when she came back and curled herself into a ball on the couch. "I'm very sorry, and I understand your grief, but it's important you think hard and try to give us any information that might be helpful. I know how attached you became to Mr. Maxwell, and it's clear he deceived you through no fault of your own."

He got out his notebook and pen. "It was known around town that your uncle was looking into Marlene Hall's death and checking into Mr. Maxwell's background, and Maxwell probably heard about it."

"We saw my uncle yesterday." Despite what they'd said, she was still sure Judd could not be the killer. If he was innocent, telling these men the truth wouldn't hurt. She explained how she and Judd had run into Ed yesterday morning on the street. "Judd made an appointment to meet my uncle at his office yesterday afternoon, but as you know, he never made it."

"Did he reschedule the appointment?"

"No. In the course of the evening, we forgot all about it." Karen blushed.

"Did your uncle call to find out why Judd missed the appointment?"

"No.... At least, I don't think so." With the detectives following, Karen got up and checked the answering machine on the kitchen phone. The message light was blinking. Her hand shook as she pressed the button.

"Karen," the deep voice of her uncle boomed out in the kitchen, "this is Uncle Ed. Your friend never showed this afternoon. Ask him if he can meet me in the office tomorrow morning. I'll be there early, but..." There was a pause, then her uncle continued, "ask him to come between six and seven. After that I'll be gone to breakfast. Bye, pumpkin."

The tape ended with a click and whirred into rewind.

"Could Maxwell have heard this message?" Rossini asked.

"I don't know." Karen had trouble understanding the question. "He, ah, he could have, I suppose. I mean, there's no way to tell because the message stays on the tape until it's erased." A little voice warned her how incriminating this sounded. "I don't think Judd had any reason to kill my uncle. You don't have any evidence it was Judd, do you?"

"I'm afraid we do, Ms. Thomas." Rossini guided her to a dining chair. "Your uncle was using his computer when he was killed. It was still turned on when we arrived. He was beginning a case report that said he'd uncovered evidence linking Maxwell with the Marlene Hall murder. Maxwell arrived earlier than your uncle expected, probably saw what he was working on and decided to silence him right then."

Karen began to shake. "But if that happened, why would Judd leave the report on the computer? Wouldn't he try to destroy the file or something?"

"Perhaps he got flustered after the killing and simply ran, or didn't know how to work the program. A screen saver was running, so maybe Maxwell didn't see the report after all—perhaps your uncle made the mistake of hinting to Maxwell what he knew. But whatever transpired in your uncle's office, there is no longer any doubt that Maxwell killed Marlene. You see, Ms. Hall's next-door neighbor returned from a week-long backpacking trip in the mountains this morning and got the message to call our office. She

witnessed a car matching the model and color of
Maxwell's arrive and park on the road below Marlene's cottage the evening of the murder. We showed
the neighbor a mug-shot lineup, and she has positively identified Judd Maxwell as the man she saw
leave the car and walk up to Marlene's house.''

A MAN SAT in a car in the dirt lane behind Karen's
house, reflecting on the progress of his work with
cool satisfaction.

He'd followed the key players, the two plain-
clothes detectives, from the murder scene downtown,
then waited almost an hour before driving past
Karen's house and doubling back to park several
doors away in the alley. Getting so close was a calculated risk, but not a great one. The gawkers had
grown predictably bored once the patrol cars left, and
the neighbors had retreated back behind their fences
where his own car would not be noticed. It was important he keep his hand on the pulse of things, to
make sure his plan continued to proceed to the de-
sired end.

The man shifted in his seat and pounded one fist
into the steering wheel. It enraged him that Maxwell
had apparently eluded arrest. It had been an unpleas-
ant shock to find his scapegoat's car missing from
the front of the house, where it had been parked just
before five when he passed on his way to Thomas's
office. Dr. Small's car and that of the detectives were
the only vehicles parked on the street. He guessed
Karen must be so distraught that the detectives had
called in her doctor to sedate her.

Karen! A picture of her dark red hair and fair skin
filled his mind, producing a twitching in his groin.

For all her pretended innocence, the man sensed she was attracted to him, the way many women he met secretly lusted after him. Karen had sorely tempted him with the unspoken invitation he read in her eyes, but she was too close to home for comfort. He'd learned that lesson well with the schemer Marlene.

He'd had no real desire to hurt Karen; that was why he had left the note on her door for her to find yesterday, accusing Judd of murder. But she hadn't taken the hint, had continued to harbor Judd in her home. By now she was sure to know too much to be allowed to live. There were too many people around the house at the moment, but he would have to return as soon as possible to dispatch her.

The neighborhood was very quiet now beneath the gray morning sky; it was a good time to leave. He started the engine, cautiously drove past Karen's yard and onto the paved street.

Why did Maxwell have to escape, damn him! Better that the police should find him and some redneck Granite jury put him away quickly. Then he could put the whole matter truly behind him, as he had done in the past when it was necessary. But from what he'd observed of Maxwell at a distance over the past few days, he was a clever one; he wouldn't be easy to catch. Where had the slippery man run to?

Then the answer occurred to him. Of course. He'd bet his reputation on it! The man grinned with evil satisfaction. How appropriate that his "perpetrator" should return to the scene of the crime. And there might be a way to turn Maxwell's instincts to his own advantage, to seal Judd's fate even more tightly.

A cunning scenario quickly unfolded in his mind. At the light, he turned a hard right onto Main Street and gunned the engine, heading for Highway 18 and Marlene Hall's cottage.

Chapter Fourteen

Judd took a quick glance at the map caught in his fist, then turned off the highway onto two-lane Hamblin Road, the street where Marlene Hall had lived.

After vaulting the fence behind Karen's house, he'd outrun the pursuing cops and lost them as he doubled back through an adjacent yard. Cautiously approaching the front of the house, he'd been surprised and grateful to find the sidewalk free of officers and his car unguarded. Apparently the local police weren't practiced in apprehending suspected murderers.

Using the local map stored in his glove compartment, he'd driven straight to Hamblin Road, staying close to the speed limit and watching for patrol cars, but the ride had been conveniently uneventful. Until now, as strange feelings came over him while he covered the last two miles to Marlene's.

Hamblin twisted and turned, gradually steepening. Like dozens of other roads in the county, it gave access to scattered log and wood-sided cabins that had originally been built as summer homes and hunting lodges, as well as newer and larger homes, some with steeply peaked roofs to shed the winter snow.

There was nothing unusual here. Except that Judd had the eerie, déjà vu feeling he'd driven up this exact stretch of road, perhaps more than once, and passed these very houses. It was the closest he'd come since the accident to remembering anything meaningful from his past. The sensation electrified him before its clear implication filled him with dread.

His neck began to prickle. He recognized it as a subconscious warning, and anxious as he was to go forward, he decided to heed it. He pulled off the road onto a dirt drive that wound into the forest. Stepping out of the car and looking about, he was almost sure he was within a mile of Marlene's place.

His vehicle safely hidden from sight, he took up a vantage point just off the road, where he waited to see if the police were following him, and tried to analyze the strange mixture of emotions within himself.

The objective detachment he'd felt so strongly yesterday was gone this morning. But instead of feeling like himself again, like the pastless, but now familiar, man he'd been the past eight days, he felt different. It was almost as though he was morphing into someone else, a self he should know even more intimately than the amnesiac Judd, but to whom he felt a complete stranger. The sensation was disturbing, but he knew he couldn't shrink back from remembering now. He must learn the truth about himself, at any cost. He put the hindering fears aside by thinking of the one thing that mattered most to him in this world: Karen.

He regretted more than anything leaving her so suddenly, and he had to remind himself for the tenth time that there had been no other way. He pictured

her abject grief when she learned about her uncle,
and wished fiercely he'd been there to comfort her.
But the sheriff's men were sure to do a good job of
protecting her—that was the one thought that comforted him. Rossini had made it clear he considered
Karen a standout for the killer's next victim, so he
would be sure to post a guard around her. If she was
in any danger from her uncle's murderer, the deputies would keep the man at bay.

Would Rossini and his sidekick succeed in con-
vincing Karen that he, Judd, was the murderer? He
thought not. Karen was so loyal, so kindhearted—so
bullheaded. That brought a flicker of a smile to his
face. It was easy to imagine her jumping forward
with the otherwise awkward alibi that he'd been with
her all night, then facing off with his accusers by
reiterating the points she'd made to him so often that
he couldn't be Marlene's murderer.

He prayed she was right.

He heard a car engine surging uphill in the distance.

A few moments later, a sheriff's vehicle appeared
around the bend. Judd held his breath and kept still
in the cover of the bushes. A middle-aged male deputy was at the wheel, a young woman beside him in
the passenger's seat.

Judd watched carefully as they passed, a frown of
puzzlement appearing on his face. The fact the siren
wasn't going was understandable: a lawman trying
to take him by surprise wouldn't announce his approach. But the light bar, always used for safety during a pursuit, had not been lit; the officer was driving
at a moderate pace; and the female passenger, in a
plaid shirt, had been attired as a civilian rather than

a deputy or detective. But it would be too much of a coincidence to find a sheriff's vehicle on Hamblin Road *not* heading for the Hall cottage.

The enigma provided a mental distraction from his emotions. But after another ninety minutes of waiting, the cruiser did not return, and Judd's restless apprehension grew unbearable. He returned to his own car and studied the map; Hamblin dead-ended about two miles up. As he'd thought, the only way for the deputy to return to the station was to pass by this point. He studied the undergrowth around him; it was incredibly thick here and dotted with poison oak.

This...premonition...that he was on the brink of turning into someone else, itched at him like a rash. It would be impossible to approach the cottage without resorting to the road, but he'd explode if he didn't do something. He'd waited long enough.

Adrenaline burned in his veins. He had to see if the sheriff's man was up at Marlene's, and if the fellow had company. Judd quickly locked his car door and strode down the lane. All his senses heightened to acute awareness as he looked both ways, then stepped out into full view on Hamblin Road.

"I WISH YOU HAD AGREED to let a deputy stay with you," said Ruth Cohen from behind the wheel as she drove toward downtown Silver Creek.

"It would have been a waste of manpower," Karen said. "I'm sure they need every available man to help track Judd. I don't think he'll come around the house again."

"Then why are we driving to a sporting goods store to buy you a gun?"

Karen couldn't give an answer that would ease her friend's mind, not without lying to her. The truth was, she'd refused a guard not because she felt safe doing so, but because she couldn't stand the thought of a stranger hanging around to witness her grief.

Mrs. Cohen had shown up as Karen's family doctor was leaving, his offer of a sedative politely but firmly refused. Mrs. Cohen, full of news of the murder and anxious to offer her comfort and assistance, had assured Dr. Small she would care lovingly for his patient. Karen would have sent her landlady away also, had she not vaguely realized that the purchase of a firearm could be a difficult transaction and that Mrs. Cohen might be of help. The wealthy woman was a bulldozer when she wanted something, for herself or one of her friends, and Karen didn't feel up to negotiating the purchase herself.

But all Karen really, desperately wanted at this moment was to crawl back home, close the drapes and turn off the phone, and give in to the pain and remorse that pressed in on her like a vise.

"I don't care for guns, myself," Mrs. Cohen said.

"Neither do I."

"I suppose that's heresy, here in hunting country."

Karen tuned out Mrs. Cohen's chatter and thought of her uncle. Perhaps his spirit was hovering protectively near her; perhaps he'd gone on to the next life to be with his brother and sister-in-law, Karen's father and mother. But if he were to try to get a message to her now, she was sure she knew what it would be: *Don't let that madman get you.*

Where had Judd gone wrong? What had made him capable of taking the lives of other human beings?

She could still hardly believe it—she'd been sure she saw so much good in him, so much desire to do the right thing. He had certainly been troubled, but not unbalanced! Had his memory returned as Uncle Ed talked to him about Marlene? Had overwhelming fear of capture made him brandish the gun? He should have realized that killing Ed was absolutely wrong, senseless. It made her heartsick to think he'd done it. But the proof against him was overwhelming.

"Karen, did you hear what I said?"

"Huh?" Would Mrs. Cohen never stop talking?

"I said, 'I wish you would accept my offer and come stay at the house with Truman and me, until they catch this kook.'"

Karen said nothing. She'd already politely declined the offer several times. Ruth apparently decided not to argue with her this time, because she started musing on another topic. "Truman was scheduled to give a lecture in New York tomorrow, but they canceled and he didn't go. I'm just as glad, because there's the maid, of course, and the gardener lives on the grounds, but with a madman on the loose, I feel safer having Truman at home." With barely a breath in between, Mrs. Cohen changed subjects again. "Do you think Judd really had amnesia, or was he only pretending?"

"I don't know. With all my training and field experience working with people, I should have been able to read him. But I still don't know what was acting and what wasn't. If you had asked me, I would have said he was a very different man." Her voice broke at that.

Mrs. Cohen regarded her with beetled brows.

"Karen, exactly what happened between you and Judd? Did you fall in love with him?"

Karen couldn't hold back the tears any longer. She dug in her purse for a tissue and held it over her face.

"You can tell me, dear. No one will blame you—the man was an expert con artist."

But Karen couldn't tell her. Not how Judd taking her in his arms last night had sent an uncontrollable thrill from her head to her toes. How utterly safe and right she'd felt with her arms around Judd's neck as he carried her to the bedroom. How fulfilled she'd been as they lay beside one another after making love, Judd kissing her eyelids with the tenderest brush of his lips. The sadness and aloneness she'd faced as a single woman had seemed forever past. In its place had been peace and joy, the depth of which she'd never known.

As the tears threatened to turn to sobs, Mrs. Cohen reached over and patted Karen's shoulder. "I'm sorry, dear, I shouldn't have asked you, not now. What a ninny I am. In a few days' time, you'll be calmer, and able to talk about it. Come on, we're almost at the store, let's think about something else."

The suggestion sounded absurd, but Karen knew Mrs. Cohen was right. If she couldn't pull herself together, she'd go home without the gun she needed. As she shifted in her seat to focus on the driver, the rich moroccan leather of the seat made a creaking sound. "This is a beautiful car," Karen said, reaching for another tissue to dry her eyes. "I don't, ah—" she gulped a hiccup "—think I've ever seen a four-by-four with leather seats before."

Ruth chuckled, and Karen sensed what an effort

the facade of levity was for her. For all her pushy ways, the flamboyant woman really was a good friend.

"I tease Truman that this sport utility vehicle has more of a plush interior than my Mercedes sedan. We both adore the smell of leather. Though the last time he had the car detailed, they used some ghastly cleaner in here. Can't you smell it?"

In her preoccupation, Karen hadn't noticed. Though she was all stuffy from crying, she obediently sniffed the air, then wrinkled her nose. "Yes, I see what you mean. It smells like disinfectant."

"Here we are," Mrs. Cohen announced.

McCauley's Sporting Goods had been a tenant of the old storefront on Main Street ever since Karen could remember, and this time of year, the shop clearly catered to fishermen. Long lines of fiberglass poles flanked the main aisle. Most of the cases seemed to be filled with fishing lures and reels. Mrs. Cohen led the way to the back counter, where a phalanx of hunting rifles was displayed on the wall. A few handguns rested in the locked case adjacent.

A man in his early forties appeared through a door to the back room. He wore a blue plaid shirt rolled up at the elbows, and he ran his hand over his balding scalp when he spotted Mrs. Cohen.

"Morning, Ruth."

"Good morning, Jimmy. Karen, this is my friend and tenant, Jimmy McCauley. Jimmy, Karen Thomas."

The owner nodded, gave a slight, professional smile. Karen returned her gaze to the guns in the case. They reminded her forcibly of her uncle's hobby, and she had to fight to keep the tears from starting again. She wondered if Jimmy had sold anything to Uncle Ed; he'd doubtless purchased ammunition here, if nothing else. How incredibly tragic it was that the objects that Ed had collected and spent so many happy hours practicing with had been the instrument of taking his life.

"Miss Thomas requires a gun," Mrs. Cohen said matter-of-factly.

The pieces displayed all looked enormous to Karen, as though they would be heavy to lift and require great hand strength to fire. "Don't you have anything…?"

"Less grotesque," Mrs. Cohen finished for her.

"I'm sorry, ladies, but we don't stock many handguns. Our trade is mostly in hunting rifles."

"Miss *Thomas,*" she emphasized, "needs something smaller. A woman's gun."

The only change in McCauley's expression was a slight forehead wrinkle of exasperation. "Ruth, I don't carry women's guns."

"Oh, my word, Jimmy McCauley, where have you been all morning?"

"In the back…doing inventory. It's been a slow morning."

"And you didn't have a radio on while you worked?"

"Yeah, I did. My shortwave. I like to listen to some of the foreign channels."

Mrs. Cohen rolled her eyes. "Karen, will you excuse us for a moment." She curtly motioned for the proprietor to follow her down the counter, then leaned across to whisper. Karen prayed her gossipy landlady wasn't going to embarrass her with a long-winded recitation of her uncle's death and Karen's connection with the suspected killer. She stared at the deer heads mounted over the gun counter and tightly balled a tissue in her fist. Thankfully Mrs. Cohen cut it short, and they returned in barely two minutes.

"I'm very sorry, Miss Thomas, about your uncle," Jimmy said. "He was a fine man, and a good customer." He cleared his throat, but from his expression he seemed to be feeling genuinely sympathetic rather than uncomfortable or awkward, and it made Karen feel just a bit better.

"I wish I had something to show you, Miss Thomas, but we just don't get any call for lighter pieces in these parts. I'd be more than happy, though, to order something for you."

"How long would that take?" Ruth asked.

"A few days. I'll put a rush on it."

"A few days!" Karen almost said, *I could be dead by then.* Panic roiled inside her. Mrs. Cohen began to protest in an outraged voice.

"Wait a minute, just wait, please, ladies. Let me think." His upraised hand moved to his chin. "You know, I think I *might* just have something that would do...yes, I'm sure it never sold. There's a little automatic I ordered a couple years ago for a customer who changed his mind. It will take me just a minute to find it in the back."

Karen's face relaxed. "That would be wonderful."

The storekeeper smiled. "I'll clean it for you and make sure it's in good working order." He started for the stockroom, then turned in the doorway. "Are you trained to use a pistol?"

"No." The ever present knot in Karen's stomach pulled tighter. She'd never fired a gun in her life, and just the thought of touching it made her feel she might be ill.

Jimmy's brow wrinkled. "You won't be able to hit the side of a barn, much less a target, unless I give you some practice. Ruth, you better turn the Closed sign around in the window."

JUDD FOUND THE DEPUTY and his female passenger on the steps of an A-frame that fronted Hamblin Road. Judd hid in the trees as the man thanked the attractive young woman for the coffee, then repeated several times that he thought she had nothing to worry about, but that she should call him immediately if anything came up or if she remembered anything else about the murder. That made Judd smile ruefully: he'd bet the deputy had been using what little authority he had to impress the woman while he dallied at her house, when he was really supposed to be out doing his job. When the patrol car drove off toward town, Judd exhaled and prayed his good luck would hold. If the sheriff's man had left two minutes earlier, he would have caught Judd on the road.

From his vantage point, he could see the mailbox with Marlene Hall's number on it. It was the next one up, on the same side of the street. Strange Rossini hadn't mentioned they had a neighbor who was a witness.

He could barely see the corner of Marlene's white clapboard cottage, about three hundred yards up the steep dirt driveway. Shrubbery grew in from the sides, and deep gullies ran down the length of the roadbed. The lane was obviously no longer used, and it would take a four-wheel drive to climb it. His wide old car would never have made it. If he'd taken Marlene's body away in his trunk, he would have had to park on Hamblin and carry her down.

He cautiously scouted up the street a bit, but there were no other police cars in sight, and the only human-manufactured sound was a shower running in one of the widely spaced homes.

He went back to get his car, in case one of the sheriff's men turned up again and he needed to make a quick escape. He drove past Marlene's mailbox and just out of sight around a bend. He parked behind a big blue Mercedes that seemed vaguely familiar, but he couldn't be sure; the coming and going of residents' vehicles hadn't seemed important while he'd kept his vigil by the road.

But now he was on full alert. He kept his eyes open as he walked back down Hamblin and turned up Marlene's driveway. An uncomfortable tightness was forming in his temples. Some sixth sense was telling him there was something up there at the cottage, something that had been waiting for him. He told himself he should have come here earlier, would have come earlier, if the police hadn't taken him in for questioning yesterday afternoon.

Subconscious fears warned him to turn around and run back down the overgrown track, but he didn't slacken his pace. Even if this place was haunted, it was time for the ghosts to be laid to rest, for the story of his past to be revealed.

The tiny cottage was in need of paint, its dirty white sides flaking badly in places, its tar-paper roof ragged and coated with green moss where adjacent pines overhung it. A surprisingly clean mullioned window with pretty lace curtains faced the road. Perspiration trickled down Judd's back as he stepped up and looked in.

It was a woman's bedroom, delicate and feminine. The bed was covered with a blue satin comforter; an open but empty suitcase lay on it. The residue of black fingerprint powder was visible on the top of the antique bird's-eye-maple dresser and around the porcelain drawer pulls. How tragic that Marlene had entered this room, perhaps full of happy anticipation, just moments before her death.

Judd grimaced as he proceeded to the next window, on the long side of the house and next to the front door. The wide picture window looked in on a knotty-pine-paneled living room. The mismatched sofa and easy chairs weren't new, but tasteful, and some pretty vases, filled with wilted flowers, were scattered on the oak tables. A swinging door painted in white enamel undoubtedly led to the kitchen.

Judd stepped back. There was a high window, perhaps over a sink, at the corner of the house; it was covered by a closed venetian blind.

His mouth went dry. He pushed the hair out of his eyes, forced his wooden limbs to move past the window and around the side of the kitchen. There was a concrete parking pad here, cracked by weeds, a rotting clothesline and two more shuttered windows. There must be a kitchen door around the back.

Sure enough, he found a two-step porch leading to a wooden door with glass cutouts, which were not curtained. Judd involuntarily paused for a moment, his heart thudding as he stared at the door. A premonition came over him that a dead body lay just beyond the threshold. His hand shook as he grasped the banister and forced himself up the steps. He cupped his hands around his eyes and moved his face to the glass.

Weak sunlight filtered through the closed blinds of the other windows onto knotty pine cabinets, tiled counters and a simple Formica dinette. He willed his gaze down to the floor; it was clean and bare. Judd breathed a sigh of relief mixed with disappointment: so this was all there was to see.

Then he saw the woman's body.

She was lying in a twisted heap where she'd collapsed, a puddle of deep red spreading out over the linoleum from the gash in her neck.

Judd was transfixed with the vision; his hand clutched at the door frame as his legs threatened to give way. And a dust storm of bizarre pictures began whirling in his head.

He cried out and squeezed his eyes shut. The pictures flashed by with dizzying speed; he knew they were snapshots of his past life. Some he didn't recognize, but others were frighteningly familiar. His temples pounded as he tried to regain control of his spinning mind, tried to slow down the images and grab on to the ones he recognized.

After some minutes, his head began to clear. He was able to pull his thoughts into patterns. Slowly a chronology of sorts began to surface.

He'd been here, of course, that fateful night. He'd hurried up the driveway to Marlene's house, intent on warning her to get out of town, and discovered to his horror that the man he'd been shadowing had beaten him here, for the bronze Jeep Cherokee was parked on the pad. With weapon drawn and running quietly as a cat, he'd circled around to this door, peered in and found Marlene newly slain.

Guilt and disbelief had overwhelmed him. For six months, he'd tracked a serial killer from Los Angeles to Seattle to Silver Creek, committed every fiber of his being to preventing the loss of another innocent young woman's life. He was an FBI agent, but this case had become more than an assignment; it had been an obsession. If he'd been more decisive, arrived only moments sooner, he could have prevented this senseless abomination.

The killer was heavily armed, and taking him without assistance would be nearly impossible. Judd's only advantage had been that the man didn't spot him. He'd followed the Cherokee, intending to stop and call for backup at the first available phone. Then…nothing.

Judd shook his head as if to dislodge the skip in his memory. The murderer. Who was he? He tried to focus on the face he'd seen as the perpetrator staggered from the house, carrying Marlene's limp body wrapped in a blanket. As the features became more detailed, Judd realized he'd seen the same man, only days ago…at Karen's house.

"Stay right there, with your hands up," a voice called behind him. "Very nice. Yes, you may turn around. Slowly!"

Judd faced a .45 revolver pointed at his chest. Without surprise, he locked eyes with Truman Cohen.

Chapter Fifteen

The short, mustached man was dressed in pressed gabardines, tasseled loafers, a silk shirt buttoned at the collar and a white cashmere golf sweater. The thought crossed Judd's mind that, had this been a movie, the dapper, erudite gentleman before him would make a perfect evil twin for Hercule Poirot. However, Judd knew from experience there was nothing comical about the demented mind behind Cohen's intense black eyes.

"Keep your hands up—I want to see what you do with them." When Judd mutely obeyed, Cohen continued, "So you did see me kill Marlene. I could tell, from your expression as you stood there just now, looking in. You see, until this moment, I wasn't sure. The first time Ruth told me there was an amnesia victim in town, and where and when they'd found you, I began to wonder. Then this morning, I had the strangest feeling you'd turn up here. Perhaps there is some kind of psychic connection between us."

With all the time Judd had spent tracking Cohen, trying to get inside the head of the serial killer, Truman might be right. Recalling the paranoia he had felt in the early days of his amnesia, that he was in danger, Judd was sure now that deep in his subconscious he had been aware of Cohen's existence all the time. A man without a memory would have been a sitting duck for a killer bent on eliminating his only witness. But for all Cohen had learned, he still seemed to be ignorant of the fact that Judd was FBI, and Judd wasn't about to say anything to tip him off.

"Why did you murder Ed Thomas?" Judd asked. "Was he on to you?"

"No, actually he hadn't connected me with Marlene." Cohen worked his tongue around his mouth, obviously tempted to go on. "We were very circumspect, you see, but my wife thought I'd been behaving in an evasive manner, so she hired Mr. Thomas to spy on me. Well, somehow he discovered I'd been seeing other women on my lecture tours, and he called last night, asking to see me. I had an early flight scheduled, so he agreed to meet me in his office before dawn. You understand, he wanted to offer me the gentlemanly way out, to allow me to tell Ruth the truth, before he gave her his report. He probably thought she would forgive me if I made a clean breast of it, but I knew better. And Ruth's income…well, let's just say it would cause certain difficulties if she decided to divorce me."

"So you shot him?"

"Thomas's gun was lying on the desk. He'd been cleaning and loading it when I arrived." Cohen's eyes flicked to the PI's revolver in his hand. "I realized I could accomplish two objectives at once—silence Thomas, and make it look as though you had done the deed. That way, the police would never believe you if you suddenly regained your memory and claimed you'd witnessed me kill Marlene."

Judd listened with sick fascination. "How could you be sure the police would blame me for Ed's murder?"

"I typed the first paragraph of a report into his computer, claiming he'd uncovered evidence that proved you killed Marlene."

"You bastard!"

Judd lunged down the steps; Cohen backed up a foot, but halted Judd with a stab of the gun. "I wouldn't insult me, if I were you, Mr. Maxwell. I'm intelligent and resourceful, but not a criminal. Marlene Hall forced me to do what I did."

Judd couldn't contain his anger. "And the other women, what about them? What crimes against your dignity did they commit that made them deserve death?"

Cohen's brows rose into the bangs of his toupee. "You know far more than is good for you, Mr. Maxwell, and you've made my decision for me. The police will theorize that guilt finally caught up with you and made you commit suicide at the scene of one of your killings, with the weapon you used from your last murder."

Neither man hesitated. Judd recognized the cold-blooded resolve in Cohen's eyes and dived for the ground as the other man pulled the trigger. The bullet scored his left arm, but Judd recovered his balance and scuttled into the trees. The second shot whizzed past and lodged in a pine trunk. Cohen cursed inelegantly and sprang after him.

Judd had reconnoitered the woods around Marlene's cottage the first day he suspected she was involved with Truman. There was a dry creek bed running between the properties down to Hamblin Road.

He cut a zigzag path through the trees, the killer following with less speed and more difficulty. A well-sighted third short missed Judd's left ear by inches and made him shy. He found the gully and slid down into it.

Judd stopped a moment to listen. There was an oath, then silence, behind him. The creek bed wasn't apparent until you got almost on top of it; it sounded as though Cohen was baffled by the sudden disappearance of his quarry. Bending low and moving as quietly as he could, Judd headed downstream.

He shimmied on his belly through the drainage pipe under Hamblin Road and climbed out into the trees on the opposite side of the roadway. His pursuer was still up somewhere on the forested hillside. Judd sprinted for his car.

A gray-haired lady in a housedress and floppy sweater stood on the porch of her home as Judd raced by. Though he doubted Cohen would fire at him before a witness, there was still a chance the woman was at risk.

"Get in the house!" he yelled, knowing he must appear a wild man, his clothes covered with dirt. The elderly gawker squeaked and retreated indoors.

Judd piled into his car. Blood from the wound on his left arm had soaked his shirt, and it was still seeping. He tore the right sleeve off with his teeth and quickly made a tourniquet. In the rearview mirror, Truman Cohen was sprinting toward him with surprising speed. Judd jammed on the ignition and threw the car in reverse. Cohen barely jumped clear, then thumped the hood of the car and screamed through the windshield at Judd. Judd threw on the brakes and turned the big car on a dime. Half expecting to hear a shot aimed at his tires, he burned rubber.

His only thought as he sped down the hill was to reach Karen before Cohen did. Truman had no way of knowing Judd had regained his memories of the murder just minutes before; in his paranoia, Cohen was sure to assume Karen knew more about the murders than she did. He was ruthlessly eliminating everyone who suspected him, and Judd was sure his love was number three on that list.

Judd had to slow for the stop sign at the foot of Hamblin; he was just turning as two sheriff's cars streaked down Highway 18 from the direction of Silver Creek, their lights flashing, and made to go up Hamblin Road. Judd sucked his breath in and prayed they'd be too preoccupied to recognize his car. He pulled onto the highway at a normal speed and checked his mirror. The deputies were making a U-turn.

"Damn." Was this where his luck would run out? He prayed for just one more break, for Karen's sake, and pushed the accelerator to the floor.

Judd had chosen the Impala as an unassuming surveillance vehicle, but he'd also modified its powerful V-8 engine himself, to enhance its pursuit capability, and he'd kept it in perfect tune. He called up every ounce of available horsepower as the patrol cars tracked him toward Silver Creek, sirens wailing. Just short of the city limit, a third sheriff's car pulled out from a side road to join the chase. The chances they would cause a wreck and hurt an innocent bystander warred with Judd's certainty that Karen's life was in danger. He slowed as much as he dared as they hit downtown.

The first traffic light was green. A woman unlocking her car on the street froze when she heard the sirens and looked up to see Judd bearing down on her. He swerved into the empty oncoming lane to signal her presence to his pursuers.

Two blocks up, the eye of the light was a stubborn, fiery red.

Judd leaned on his horn. From the middle of the intersection, a teenager in a foreign compact saw him coming. The boy leaned forward and put on speed just in time to avoid the oncoming juggernaut.

Judd exhaled in relief as he swept by. Then he saw the truck.

The driver of the logging truck seemed oblivious to other traffic as he slowly pulled across Main Street. The trailer, stacked with unmilled logs, filled Judd's view through the windshield. He shouted as he crushed the brakes and raised his injured arm in front of his face.

FOUR BLOCKS BACK, Truman Cohen saw the massive truck and heard the frantic squeal of locked tires leaving their tread on asphalt. He smiled with self-justification as he turned off Main Street and swiftly threaded his way through the residential section toward Karen Thomas's house.

KAREN REMOVED the little silver Beretta from her handbag and set it gingerly on a place mat on the dining table. A moment later, she moved the gun to the coffee table, stood back and looked at it, then slid the sports section of the newspaper over it. She frowned, moved her hand to her stomach and rubbed.

How tired she was. Too tired to sleep. Too upset to sleep.

She had this instinctive feeling she couldn't let herself lose consciousness until the world had righted itself, if just a bit. But when would that be? How could life possibly ever feel normal again?

She knew she'd go crazy if she didn't get her mind to rest, if she couldn't think about something else for a while.

"You're unusually quiet this morning," she said, turning her attention to Trouble in the wrought-iron cage. The cockatiel paced on his perch but refused to greet her. His topped-off food bowl was untouched.

Karen leaned closer. His tail didn't look right.

"Trouble, what's the matter?" Karen opened the door and extended her index finger toward the bird, who stepped warily away.

"Come on, sweetie," Karen coaxed. There was a pinkish, bare spot in the feathers over his heart. Trouble allowed her to press his stomach with her hand, then finally raised a hesitant foot and climbed on. Karen carefully withdrew the parrot from the cage.

"What happened to you?" His graceful, V-shaped tail was truncated by a good three inches and ended in a blunt stub. A handful of downy breast and tail feathers lay on the floor of the cage, one long plume tipped in blood.

"You're pulling your feathers out. Oh, Trouble!" Karen wanted to comfort the bird, but had no idea how. She stroked his head as tears filled her throat. "I know you miss Judd, but he's not worth it. I promise, I'll take care of you from now on. We don't need him, neither of us do! You'll see."

The bird gave a sad little cheep, obviously no more convinced by her words than she was.

THE REAR OF JUDD'S CAR skidded forward in an arc; the left rear fender slammed into the rear axle of the logging truck. The three police cars were almost on top of him. Judd hit the accelerator; the tires spun free, miraculously unimpeded by the twisted fender, and the Impala shot back down the street the way Judd had come.

The braking cop cars fishtailed past him and piled into the truck like dominos. Judd slalomed past shocked motorists who had come to a standstill, and disappeared down an alley.

KAREN SLOWLY STIRRED a teaspoon of honey into her tea. A sudden pounding sound made her jerk; hot liquid spilled over the kitchen counter.

Judd stood ten feet from her, on the sunporch, hammering on the glass door to the living room. ''Karen, let me in!''

''Oh, no.'' Karen flattened herself against the counter, trying in vain to disappear from his line of sight behind the kitchen door frame. It took her a moment to remember the phone on the wall beside her, to reach for it and punch in 911. When no one answered, she finally realized there was no dial tone. She flicked the button, but the line was dead.

The pounding and shouting stopped abruptly. Karen looked; the sunporch was empty. Should she make a break for it? Judd had probably anticipated that and would catch her the moment she stepped outside! On unsteady legs, she raced to the coffee table, grabbed the little automatic pistol and ducked into the central hallway. She closed the doors to the bathroom and bedroom, held the gun against her stomach and strained to hear above the rasp of her own breathing.

There was a sound of breaking glass from behind the bedroom door. Every muscle in her body froze in terror. Would she be able to move, to fire? She forced her arms out in front of her, squared her body to face the bedroom door. The light was dim here in the center of the house. Her eyes stood out in her head, fastened on the old brass door handle in the gloom.

Was the knob turning? Maybe…yes? As if in slow motion, the door swung open. It was him.

"Karen."

Karen shut her eyes tight.

"No!" They spoke the word simultaneously, and their voices were in turn drowned out by the deafening report of the gun.

Karen stumbled back against the wall, and her eyes flew open. Judd was staring at her with wild disbelief. His arms flew up to his chest, spasmed across a ghastly red stain on his shirt, then he fell forward onto the carpet.

In horror, Karen screamed and dropped the automatic. She had been forced to stop him, but she couldn't go on if she had killed him. Half-afraid he was still conscious and might suddenly come alive to grab for her, half-afraid he was dead, she started toward him with one shaking arm outstretched. He didn't move, and both her fear of him and her hope dwindled. She hesitated only a second longer before falling on her knees beside him, her life shattered along with Judd's body.

"I must say, Karen, you did that rather well."

She looked up. Truman Cohen stood, a gun in his hand, at the entrance to the hallway. *He's come to help me,* she thought.

"I'm glad I took the time to cut your phone line. It was a fortunate delay."

Karen's mind felt fuzzy with shock. "Wha—what?"

"I was afraid Judd was going to escape both me *and* the police—I never dreamed you'd be the one to finish him off, my dear. Very convenient. It will look as though you and Maxwell shot one another as he broke in. Get up, please." When Karen didn't respond, he barked, "Get up!"

Though Karen's mind was too tortured to comprehend all that he said, she realized he meant the gun for her, not Judd. She rose unsteadily to her feet.

"Around here, come past me." Truman herded her by and backed himself up to where Judd lay. "I'll try to make this as painless as possible."

A shadow shot up from the floor behind Truman Cohen and slammed into his arm. The gun flew to the floor; Cohen gathered his wits with remarkable speed and dived after it. Simultaneously Judd lunged past him and reached for the revolver.

Karen backed out of their way as the two men wrestled on the floor for the gun. She couldn't see the pistol between the two grunting, cursing men. Then a muffled shot cracked out.

Judd's body slammed against the wall. A long, drawn-out moment later, Truman Cohen rolled from his side onto his back, unconscious.

Judd got up on all fours and shook his head as if to clear it. Elation broke through the fog of Karen's mind, and she rushed to help him to his feet. Somewhere in her subconscious, pieces were falling into place, giving her the signal that everything would be all right now.

"Thank goodness," she gasped. "Are you hurt?"

"No, you missed me completely. Lesson number one, Karen, never attempt to hit a target with your eyes closed. The blood is from my arm, but it's just a flesh wound Cohen gave me."

"Thank goodness. But if I didn't hit you, why did you fall down?"

"If I'd kept coming, you could hardly have missed me at point-blank range. I knew the best way to keep you from firing again was to play possum. That, and I thought I saw a movement behind you that could be Cohen. Letting him think I was out of the picture gave me the advantage of surprise."

Karen looked down at Truman. "Is he dead?"

"No, he's still breathing." He bent to inspect Cohen's chest more closely. "He killed Marlene and at least two other women he met while on lecture tours in Los Angeles and Seattle. And—I'm so sorry, sweetheart—when your uncle got onto him, Cohen killed him, too."

Karen gasped and pushed her fist into her mouth; Judd rose and quickly wrapped his good arm around her shoulders. "It's over now. Come on, let's find a phone that works and call the paramedics."

As they stepped into the entrance hall, Karen got another shock. The front door exploded inward, and two men in suits with guns at the ready flew into their faces. "Freeze, FBI!"

The man in front lowered his gun. Incongruously,

his face relaxed into a wreath of smiles. Karen thought she must be dreaming. "All right, Special Agent Maxwell," he boomed, "where in Hades have you been for the last nine days?"

Chapter Sixteen

"You're an FBI agent?"

"Yes." Judd grinned down at Karen. "Something I forgot to tell you, along with a lot of other things. I got my memory back, up at Marlene Hall's place this morning. That's where I ran into Truman."

The agents were busy with Cohen. One did an examination while the other called for the paramedics on a cellular phone.

"Nasty shoulder wound," the lead agent said. "Here, Arthur, you better keep some pressure on it until the ambulance arrives."

Judd introduced her to Special Agent Bob Engels from the Los Angeles field office.

"When you didn't check in for so long, and we couldn't raise you on the phone, we got worried," Engels explained, "so I decided I'd better come looking for you myself."

"I'm sorry I alarmed you, Bob, but I've got one heck of a reason, if you're able to believe it. Let's sit down, and I'll tell you."

They settled in the living room, Karen gratefully leaning back on the cushions while Judd sat forward and laced his fingers.

"To begin with, Cohen struck again," Judd began. "His wife owns a restaurant property outside of Silver Creek where the victim, Marlene Hall, worked. I was having trouble finding any evidence in town against Cohen, and had almost decided I was on the wrong track, when I learned he was secretly seeing Marlene. The afternoon of the sixteenth, I got a bad feeling, so I decided to warn Marlene about Cohen. I scraped together enough cash to send her safely out of town for a few days. Unfortunately I arrived just moments too late."

Judd cleared his throat before continuing. "As you know, I've worked my share of crime scenes, but for some reason this one really got to me. I was trailing Cohen on his way to dispose of the body when I blacked out. The next thing I knew, I woke up in a hospital in Granite with amnesia."

Bob Engels's chin hit his chest. "Holy Toledo. You *are* kidding?"

"No. This is one for that Bureau memoir we keep threatening to write. And what's more, I've been the sheriff's prime suspect ever since the murder. My wallet and my briefcase—with my badge and all the case paperwork in it—were stolen from the front seat of my car while I was unconscious. Remember, Karen," he said, looking at her, "when you drove me home to my apartment, I said I thought something vital was missing, something that would help me remember. It was the briefcase."

Karen nodded, and Judd turned back to his fellow agent. "Still, the local authorities should have known as soon as they saw my name that I was the undercover Fed working in their jurisdiction."

Bob shook his head. "They had no idea, and I'll

tell you why. You remember our supervisor had a heart attack right after you were assigned here? Well, he wasn't feeling well for some time before that, I guess he had trouble concentrating, and he never set up the liaison with the local authorities."

Judd looked startled, but he said, "Well, that explains a lot of things." He turned to Karen and picked up her hand. "Unfortunately Marlene Hall wasn't Cohen's only victim. This morning—"

"Bob," Agent Jones called from the hall, "I think the medics are here."

"Okay." Bob jumped up and motioned to Judd to join him. "Will you excuse us, Miss Thomas? Thanks."

Karen had listened to the two men, too stunned, too relieved that Judd was alive and well to say anything. She remained on the couch, out of the way, while the paramedics worked on Truman, and then the Granite detectives and some other police officers arrived and Judd went out to meet them.

When they had carried Truman out on a stretcher, Judd ran back inside. He zippered his suitcase and plucked his leather bomber jacket off the chair. He was clearly preoccupied as he slapped his pocket for his keys.

"They're taking Cohen to St. Mary's in Granite," he said to Karen. "I'm going to follow the ambulance and have a doctor look at my arm while I'm there. Special Agent Jones will stay with you for a while. Will you be okay by yourself tonight?"

Things were moving so quickly, Karen felt she didn't have time to think, but she answered, "Yes, I'm fine."

"I'll call you later, and I'll come by tomorrow and

get the rest of my things. Perhaps you wouldn't mind watching Trouble for me for a few days.''

"Judd, we've got to haul!'' Bob Engels yelled from the doorway.

Karen tried to smile as Judd left her with not so much as a backward glance.

KAREN BARELY SAW JUDD for the next five days. She was kept occupied making the funeral arrangements, briefing one of her co-workers who offered to take her appointments for the week and receiving condolence calls and visits from friends.

Judd couldn't get away on Monday, so he left a message on Karen's answering machine asking how she was and saying he would send a police clerk to collect his storage boxes. The murderer's wound, though serious, had been treated in time and was not life threatening. Because Cohen was expected to make a full recovery, Judd as the lead investigator was responsible for building the case against him and filing the necessary paperwork to have him indicted. This required him to shuttle between Silver Creek and the major cities where Truman Cohen's other victims had lived.

Tuesday, two days after the shooting, Karen shared a brief cup of coffee with Judd at the Granite County Hall of Justice following her making a formal statement.

It seemed almost surreal to her to be sitting in the same crowded cafeteria that had been deserted only a few nights before while she waited for Judd during his interrogation. Then he had been a suspected murderer; now he was a respected FBI man, responsible for apprehending an elusive killer.

Judd's mind was clearly on the case as he absently sipped his coffee. Karen didn't know how to begin, but there was something that needed saying so badly, she couldn't put it off any longer.

"Judd."

"Yes?" His gaze came around to focus on her.

"I have to tell you how sorry I am…how embarrassed and ashamed, that I lost faith in you last Sunday. Trying to shoot you was the most insane mistake I ever made."

Judd's brows lifted in surprise, and he raised a hand to stop her. "You don't have to apologize, Karen. You did the right thing. If I'd been in your place and the police had presented me with the same evidence, I would have shot in self-defense, too."

She started to speak, to tell him how devastated she would have been if she'd killed or permanently maimed him, but he wouldn't let her.

"Never apologize for refusing to be a victim, okay? The case is closed."

As she took a swallow of her coffee, she felt much relieved. Knowing that Judd didn't bear a grudge against her, she was free now to ask him about his personal life, if there was any special woman waiting for him back home, but she realized she just didn't feel up to it. And, she admitted, she was too afraid of what he might answer.

"Mr. Maxwell." A uniformed deputy approached their table. "The sheriff would like to see you right away."

Judd squeezed her shoulder briefly before leaving.

Late the next morning, Judd stood beside her at her uncle's grave site. He was solemn and supportive during the service, taking her elbow to help her into the limousine, briefly putting a brotherly arm around her as the casket was lowered into the earth. But nothing in his speech or actions indicated he felt anything for her beyond compassion and a shared sense of grief at Ed's untimely passing.

And that was when she began to become concerned. It had been easy to put her feelings and thoughts about Judd on hold early in the week. But as the weekend approached, when he hadn't called or made any attempt to meet with her to discuss their relationship, she grew worried.

She didn't know which motel he and the other FBI agents were staying in, and tracking him down through the personnel at the hall of justice might be difficult since he was on the run. But she was almost ready to make the call when the phone rang about dinnertime on Friday.

"Karen? This is Judd. I'm sorry I haven't called you sooner, but I've been tied up."

His frustrated sigh, or was it merely a tired one, came over the line.

"How's my cockatiel?"

"He's fine, though I think he misses you," Karen said, trying to relax. "You'll be glad to hear my cat finally showed up."

"Oh, yeah?" He gave a chuckle that sounded forced, almost bored. "How are they getting along?"

The amusing story Karen had saved, of the tabby's first, incredulous sighting of the bird, died in her throat. "They're, ah, fine, just fine."

"Listen, things are winding up here and I've got to report back to the field office in Los Angeles tomorrow. I wonder if I could stop by in a few hours."

"Are you in Granite?"

"Yes, I'll try to be there by eight, if that's convenient."

"Yes, that's fine."

Karen hung up the phone. Her heart leaped at the thought of seeing Judd again—it seemed more like a week than two days since they'd last spoken. But it was hard to tell what his intentions were from what he'd said. In fact, he'd seemed more preoccupied than happy. Was his call going to be an obligatory visit to say goodbye before he left Silver Creek, for all intents and purposes, for good?

The very real possibility froze her. She sat down at the dining table, too numb with anxiety to think for a few minutes. She wished now she'd kept him on the phone longer, thought to ask what his intentions were. She had no idea how he felt about her since his memory had returned. Perhaps he'd been too embarrassed to tell her their romantic involvement had been a mistake. Perhaps he felt they were strangers to one another, and assumed she felt the same way. The only thing she had begun to feel fairly sure of was that he wasn't married: he would have come out and told her if he was.

She had to talk things out with him, but how long would she have for conversation? Would he even come in for coffee if she asked, or would he be in too much of a hurry to get away and pack?

She felt unbearably jumpy and couldn't stay seated. The next two hours promised to be torturously long.

Instinct led her to the kitchen. She hadn't thought once all afternoon about food, but now she wanted to keep busy. She pulled hamburger and Italian sausage from the freezer, half an onion and a wrinkled bell pepper from the crisper. She began making spaghetti sauce.

Chopping the vegetables helped her calm down. She just couldn't picture the "new" Judd as a stranger, much as anyone might tell her he was. She still felt in her bones she knew the man well.

True, he undoubtedly had a full, important life far away in a big city, a life she'd known nothing about until a few days ago. But her basic instincts about him had been proved correct. He wasn't an aimless drifter. He was someone she'd subconsciously identified with, a man who felt connected with other human beings and responsible for their welfare in a very profound way. A man whose psyche had had to protect him from his own shattering guilt when he could not save the life of an innocent stranger. How Karen loved him for his humanity, his vulnerability. And how scared she was.

It would be an ironic tragedy, wouldn't it, if she'd finally found the one man she could love and respect, only to lose him?

She should face the possibility that Judd might very well feel differently, that he might not see her fitting into the life he'd suddenly recovered. There was no denying that his haste to move to a motel and his complete absorption with his assignment were bad signs. From what she'd seen, Judd was incredibly dedicated to the Bureau, and *any* romantic relationship might be of less importance to him than his work. Perhaps the need he'd shown for her love and support had been only a temporary aberration, caused entirely by the strange circumstances he'd been thrown into.

As she stirred the sauce, she told herself she *could*

be understanding about this. She could tell herself their affair had been a momentary thing and to not make a fuss. She could shake Judd's hand and wish him well and quietly crawl away to nurse her broken heart. She *could.*

But she wasn't going to! Karen slam-dunked an empty can into the recycling bin. She wasn't going to let him go, and it didn't matter if Judd Maxwell lived in Los Angeles or in Tombouctou, or if she could continue her social work career in Granite or had to give it up. She didn't want to let Judd go without a fight, and she wasn't going to!

It was a pity the only ingredients she had on hand were for a pasta dinner, but it was too late to run to the store for filet mignon. Karen wiped her hands on a towel and headed for the china cabinet to get out the damask tablecloth and the crystal.

JUDD CAUGHT HER by surprise. She'd intended to go change out of her sweats into a dress when the garlic bread got too close to the broiler, charred black, and she had to start over again with the other half of the loaf. She heard Judd's car pull up outside and raced to light the candles and start some mood music on the tape player.

When he didn't come in immediately, Karen got nervous. If he thought better of it and drove away, she'd never make it through the night.

Judd climbed out of the Impala as Karen came around the front of the car to greet him. "Hi," she said.

He didn't answer, and she strained to catch his expression in the shadows cast by the streetlight.

Karen's throat constricted. Used to being assertive

on behalf of others, she suddenly felt ill at ease exercising her own rights. This was going to be much harder than she'd thought! She knew she should reach out and touch his shoulder, say, *Judd, we need to talk.* But instead, she folded her arms tightly across her chest and said with forced cheeriness, "Have you had any dinner?"

"No. Yes. Actually I had something to eat before I left the city."

An obvious lie. His stomach was probably rumbling from both hunger and a guilty desire to wrap things up with her and run. It *was* worse than she'd thought. What if he was living with another woman or engaged? How embarrassing. Why hadn't she wised up the moment he moved out?

She followed him to the house, barely listening as he shared with her some annoying, though not serious, legal development in the Cohen case.

This was awful! Judd was going to feel like a heel when he saw the romantic atmosphere she'd prepared, and she was going to look like a lovesick fool. She wished she could run ahead, grab up the tablecloth with the fine china and all and toss it out on the sunporch.

Judd strode ahead of her into the dimly lit living room, immediately spotted the flaming candelabra on the dining table, and said, "What's all this?"

The ridiculous thought came to her she could tell him she was waiting for another date.

"I, well, I felt like cooking...." She rambled on like an utter idiot, saying she knew not what. His motionless back gave her a terrible, sick feeling in her stomach. If only the earth would open up!

"This is wonderful," he said in a hushed tone. He

stepped to the table, touched the white cloth and a gleaming fork with his fingertips. Karen came up beside him, and when he turned to her, she couldn't tell if it was the flickering of the tapers or if moisture glistened in the corner of his eye. He inhaled deeply and asked, "What are you making?"

Karen twisted the hem of her sweatshirt. "It's only spaghetti sauce. My grandmother's recipe, though. It's really good."

Judd reached out and put his hands on her shoulders. She wanted to stare at the carpet, afraid her heart was in her eyes, but he softly spoke her name. She had to face him, had to try to divine what he was thinking.

The angular lines of his features were softened by the light, but she couldn't mistake his sober, almost worried expression. A band around Karen's chest squeezed the air from her lungs.

"Karen." His gaze seemed to be searching her. "I realize this is harder for you than for me, because ever since we met, I've been able to get to know you and to learn about your background, while my life was a mystery to you, and even to myself, until last Sunday. But if you're willing to take my word for it, I can assure you we're more alike than you realize."

The tightness in her chest eased, and a tingling began at the base of her spine. Did she dare to hope? She drank in the sensual curve of his mouth, the perfect whiteness of his teeth.... She couldn't help it. Every part of her wanted to reach up around his neck, stand on tiptoe and kiss him.

He continued, "I've been sick of southern California and the frequent traveling for some time, and the weeks I've spent here in Silver Creek have made

me realize I want to stay. In fact, I had a long talk
with the district attorney and the sheriff this afternoon, and they've offered me the job of managing
their criminal investigations division.... Darn it,
Karen—'' he slid his hands up her neck to cradle her
cheeks ''—it's so incredible just to be with you
again, you're making me lose my train of thought.''

An indescribable feeling thrilled through her.
''Lose it, then,'' she breathed, and his mouth came
down on hers, and their arms were around each other.

He was delicious and warm and strong and utterly
wonderful. She yielded with joy as he pressed her
upper body into his chest, wanting to give him more,
never wanting to stop.

''My sweet woman.'' He emitted a husky groan,
kissed the side of her mouth, then her cheek. ''I'm
never going to get through this if you don't have
some mercy on me.''

Karen giggled and released her tight hold on him.
His face was handsomely dark with passion. He
reached inside his coat, pulled out a little box covered in white velvet. ''What I'm trying to say is,
Karen Thomas, I love you, and will you marry me?''

''Oh, Judd.'' Karen laughed and the tears
squeezed out. ''You sounded so strange on the
phone, and just now...I didn't know what to think.''

Judd tried to look contrite, but the downward tug
of his mouth had to compete with an urge to grin.
The beam won, and he swept his arm behind her
knees and picked her up.

''I know,'' he said, carrying her to the sofa and
setting her like a doll on his lap. ''I'm sorry, I was
simply a little nervous about seeing you. I wanted to
talk to you, about us, the day after it all happened,

but you had so much to deal with, it just didn't seem right to load you down with one more thing. Then I started getting tugged in fifty directions by the Bureau and the D.A.'s office. Today I reached the point where I couldn't stand being apart from you a minute longer. In fact, I would have been here sooner, but I had to make a stop on the way." He raised the ring box in his left hand. "I walked around downtown Granite until I found a jewelry store that looked just right."

Karen tore her gaze from the box and tried to conceal her girlish excitement. "They roll up the sidewalks at five. I'm surprised you found anyone open."

"They weren't. I got the phone number of the alarm company from the security sticker in the window and had them call the owner at home. He was a little reluctant to come down—until I explained what I wanted."

Judd reached around Karen to raise the velvet lid.

Fire leaped out and dazzled Karen's vision. A large central diamond was flanked by two slightly smaller diamonds, all in an exquisite filigree setting. It was the most elegant engagement ring she could imagine.

Judd spoke softly as they stared at it. "It was after I bought this that it struck me. I sat in my car thinking how the diamonds reminded me of you, how you're so uniquely beautiful and strong and compassionate, a very rare and special woman." He guided her head to his shoulder and began gently stroking her hair. "I started to worry I'd been too overconfident, that you might not grant me the greatest favor of my life. I must have looked as rattled as I felt when I drove up."

He fell silent, his hands frozen, the ring still nestled in its box. After a few moments, she drew back to look at him. Why was he so sad? Why didn't he put the ring on her finger?

He cleared his throat. "You still haven't given me an answer, Miss Thomas." His gaze met hers, filled with desperate hope. "Will you marry me?"

Karen blushed to the roots of her fiery hair. "Oh yes, Judd! Of course I will. A thousand times yes."

He put the engagement band on her finger as tears of joy silently coursed down her cheeks. She modeled the ring, her eyes shifting in wonder from the diamonds, to his dear face and back and forth again. She almost couldn't believe what was happening.

She hugged his neck. "This is such a wonderful moment, darling. I'll never forget it."

Judd squeezed her, fully prepared to never let her go. "I won't forget it, either, sweetheart. And that's a promise."

V™ SILHOUETTE

INTRIGUE™

COMING NEXT MONTH

MARRIED IN HASTE Dani Sinclair

McKella Patterson had barely said 'I do' before her groom
disappeared and a stranger swept her off her feet—and out of
the way of a speeding truck. He told her his name was Greg
Wyman—and that her marriage was a fake. But could she
accept this stranger's protection?

FIRST-CLASS FATHER Charlotte Douglas

Heather Taylor had never told cop Dylan Wade that she'd had
his baby. But now her son had been kidnapped, and Dylan was
the only one who could help her find him... Dylan had said he
still loved her—but that could change when he found out that
the missing boy was his son...

NO ORDINARY MAN Suzanne Brockmann

Jess Baxter's new tenant Rob Carpenter was definitely the
sexiest man she'd ever met! But no matter how hard she tried,
he wouldn't let her get to know him. Then the murders
started—all women who looked like her. And the profile of the
killer matched Rob... Was he being set-up—or was he a
murderer?

SEND ME A HERO Rita Herron

Detective Nathan Dawson had been warned about Veronica
Miller's 'false alarms' but instinct told him she wasn't
imagining things. Someone *was* stalking her. And he was
going to risk his job—and his heart—to keep her safe. Only
first they had to uncover the truth about a night she couldn't
remember...

COMING NEXT MONTH FROM

Sensation
A thrilling mix of passion, adventure and drama

A MAN LIKE MORGAN KANE Beverly Barton
RANCHER'S CHOICE Kylie Brant
MAN OF THE HOUR Maura Seger
OWEN'S TOUCH Lee Magner

Special Edition
Compelling romances packed with emotion

SNOW BABY Cathy Gillen Thacker
WARRIOR'S WOMAN Laurie Paige
A MOTHER FOR JEFFREY Trisha Alexander
STRANDED ON THE RANCH Pat Warren
THE COWBOY TAKES A WIFE Lois Faye Dyer
PARTNERS IN MARRIAGE Allison Hayes

Desire
Provocative, sensual love stories

BELOVED Diana Palmer
THE BABY CONSULTANT Anne Marie Winston
THE LONE RIDER TAKES A BRIDE Leanne Banks
COWBOYS ARE FOR LOVING Marie Ferrarella
A SPARKLE IN THE COWBOY'S EYES Peggy Moreland
OVERNIGHT HEIRESS Modean Moon

FREE

2 BOOKS
AND A SURPRISE GIFT!

We would like to take this opportunity to thank you for reading this Silhouette® book by offering you the chance to take TWO more specially selected titles from the Intrigue™ series absolutely FREE! We're also making this offer to introduce you to the benefits of the Reader Service™—

- ★ FREE home delivery
- ★ FREE monthly Newsletter
- ★ FREE gifts and competitions
- ★ Exclusive Reader Service discounts
- ★ Books available before they're in the shops

Accepting these FREE books and gift places you under no obligation to buy; you may cancel at any time, even after receiving your free shipment. Simply complete your details below and return the entire page to the address below. *You don't even need a stamp!*

YES! Please send me 2 free Intrigue books and a surprise gift. I understand that unless you hear from me, I will receive 4 superb new titles every month for just £2.70 each, postage and packing free. I am under no obligation to purchase any books and may cancel my subscription at any time. The free books and gift will be mine to keep in any case.

19EC

Ms/Mrs/Miss/Mr ....Initials ....
BLOCK CAPITALS PLEASE

Surname...

Address...

....

....Postcode ....

Send this whole page to:
THE READER SERVICE, FREEPOST CN81, CROYDON, CR9 3WZ
(Eire readers please send coupon to: P.O. Box 4546, Dublin 24.)

Offer valid in UK and Eire only and not available to current Reader Service subscribers to this series. We reserve the right to refuse an application and applicants must be aged 18 years or over. Only one application per household. Terms and prices subject to change without notice. Offer expires 31st December 1999. As a result of this application, you may receive further offers from Harlequin Mills & Boon and other carefully selected companies. If you would prefer not to share in this opportunity please write to The Data Manager at the address above.

Silhouette is a registered trademark used under license.
Intrigue is being used as a trademark.

MARIE FERRARELLA

invites you to meet

THE CUTLER FAMILY
*Five siblings who find love in the
most unexpected places!*

In July:
COWBOYS ARE FOR LOVING

In September:
WILL AND THE HEADSTRONG FEMALE

In November:
THE LAW AND GINNY MARLOW

And in January 2000:
A MATCH FOR MORGAN

▼ SILHOUETTE
DESIRE®